"Your daughter will be fine," Jeb said. "She's had a very good teacher."

"I just want so much for her," Megan said, a flicker of doubt clouding her eyes.

"Do you ever think about wanting for yourself, Megan?"

She looked up at him. "What could I possibly want? I've already been so blessed. Let's just say it didn't always seem like things would turn out so well for me—for Faith and me."

He held her gaze. "Want to get some air? It's the first really warm night we've had since I got here."

Her hesitation was brief but undeniable. "Let me just get my sweater. I left it upstairs and…"

"No need," he said, removing his suit jacket and placing it around her shoulders. "Got you covered."

Books by Anna Schmidt

Love Inspired

Caroline and the Preacher
A Mother for Amanda
The Doctor's Miracle
Love Next Door
Matchmaker, Matchmaker...
Lasso Her Heart
Mistletoe Reunion
Home at Last
The Pastor Takes a Wife

Love Inspired Historical

Seaside Cinderella
Gift from the Sea
An Unexpected Suitor
A Convenient Wife

ANNA SCHMIDT

is an award-winning author of more than twenty-five works of historical and contemporary fiction. She is a two-time finalist for the coveted RITA® Award from Romance Writers of America as well as four times a finalist for the *RT Book Reviews* Reviewer's Choice Award. The most recent *RT Book Reviews* Reviewer's Choice Nomination was for her 2008 Love Inspired Historical novel, *Seaside Cinderella,* which is the first of a series of four historical novels set on the romantic island of Nantucket. Critics have called Anna "a natural writer, spinning tales reminiscent of old favorites like *Miracle on 34th Street.*" Her characters have been called "realistic" and "endearing" and one reviewer raved, "I love Anna Schmidt's style of writing!"

The Pastor Takes a Wife
Anna Schmidt

Steeple
Hill®

Published by Steeple Hill Books™

STEEPLE HILL BOOKS

Steeple Hill®

Recycling programs for this product may not exist in your area.

ISBN-13: 978-0-373-87604-4

THE PASTOR TAKES A WIFE

www.SteepleHill.com

Printed in U.S.A.

Blessed are the merciful, for they shall
have mercy shown them.
—*Matthew* 5:7

To my courageous and ever-resourceful "sisters" in Iraq and Rwanda.

Chapter One

Having accepted his first pastoral position, in the small northern Wisconsin town of Singing Springs, Jeb was well aware that he had his work cut out for him. As a former businessman he couldn't help but focus on growing the congregation and that didn't sit all that well with some.

"We're fine," one woman had assured him. "Just fine the way we are. You just keep giving us inspiring words like you did today and we'll be just fine."

He folded his hands behind his head and frowned up at a whiteboard where he'd drawn an intricate pie chart of the demographics of the congregation.

"Pastor?"

Jeb swiveled in the old wooden desk chair he'd inherited from his predecessor. A woman was standing in the doorway, the sunlight behind her casting her features in shadow, and yet he felt as if he recognized her.

"At your service," he said, standing and extending his hand in welcome.

She stepped forward, shifting what appeared to be a large afghan to one hip, and accepted his handshake.

Her hand was slender with long fingers that wrapped around his in a firm no-nonsense grip. He remembered seeing her in church the previous Sunday—his first sermon. She'd sat in the third pew on the left with Reba Treadwell.

"Hi," she said, her voice a little breathless. Was that exertion or anxiety? The last thing he wanted to do was make people nervous. "I'm Megan Osbourne. I work for Reba Treadwell? At the Cranberry Hill Inn?"

Each statement ended in a questioning lilt, as if she were uncertain of the information.

"Of course." Jeb hurried to move a pile of books and papers from the only other chair in the cluttered office. "I'm afraid I haven't quite gotten settled in yet. It's quite a change from Chicago. Please, have a seat."

"I didn't mean to interrupt. I just stopped by to bring you this afghan." She handed him the bundle. "Reba was concerned that you might not be prepared for how cold the nights can be up here, even in May."

He accepted the afghan, then glanced around for an empty space to put it. Finally he settled for draping it over the back of his chair. "Mrs. Treadwell strikes me as one of those natural-born nurturers."

Megan Osbourne perched on one corner of the straight-backed chair, her hands folded in her lap. She looked like a kid called to the principal's office, unsure of exactly what to expect. And yet on closer examination he saw that she was definitely no kid. She was certainly approaching her mid-thirties. Maybe it was the cap of hair the color of winter wheat, or the eyes, large and blue, or the skin devoid of makeup as far as he could tell, that made her appear so youthful.

Jeb sat down across from her. "Well, Mrs. Osbourne…"

"It's Megan," she interrupted, and seemed about to say more, but only added, "Just Megan."

"Well, Megan, it's really nice to meet you. I have to admit though, in the last couple of days I've been meeting so many people, it's been like a whirlwind."

"It'll taper off," she assured him, and he knew she was trying to reassure him. But then she gasped and covered her mouth with one hand. "I didn't mean because people would lose interest…I only meant…everyone thinks you're great. You should have heard people raving about your first sermon."

"But there is a curiosity factor to be considered, right?"

She nodded. "It's natural."

"So my job—at least part of it—is to get people in the habit of coming to church regularly before that curiosity factor wears off. Actually, I was working on that very thing." He pointed to the pie chart. "Maybe you could help me with a little brainstorming here."

Her blue eyes widened and she looked directly at him for the first time since she'd entered his study.

"I'll try, but I seriously doubt that…"

"Great." He stepped up to the whiteboard. "You see, I may be new at this ministry thing, but I'm beginning to discover that in some ways it's not all that different from my previous career."

"You were the CEO of a major corporation," she said, then hastened to add, "Reba was on the search committee and, well, it was only natural that she'd talk about the various candidates. We live in the same house and work at the same place, after all." She leaned in for a closer look at the pie chart. "What seems to be the problem?"

"It's the way these different age groups respond to

me—or any minister, I suspect. When you're the CEO of a business you get used to people walking on eggshells whenever you're around. In fact, that can work to your advantage. But a minister needs to connect. If I can't build relationships with people in the church, then how can I expect them to trust me as their spiritual leader?"

"But that's what being a minister is—I mean, we already accept you as our spiritual leader. That's why we hired you."

"But I want to earn it, Megan. More than that, I want to grow this church just like I once built my business. Not for the glory of it, but because this church has been here for generations and I don't want it to die on my watch." He tapped the pie chart with one end of a dry-erase marker. "Look at this. Right now our congregation is getting older, with very few people your age coming along."

"Singing Springs is an aging community. Young people tend to go off to college, or move to the city for a better job or…"

"You didn't leave."

To his surprise, she stood up and pulled her cardigan sweater closer, as if she had a sudden chill. "The demographics will shift once the summer residents start arriving. You'll see. You've got nothing to worry about." She edged toward the door. "Oh, I almost forgot. Reba asked me to invite you to her house behind the inn for supper tonight." She smiled and added, "She thinks you could use a good home-cooked meal."

Jeb laughed. "I won't turn that down, but could I take a rain check? I have an appointment over in Boulder Junction tonight."

"Sure. I'll have Reba call you." She started back down the hall toward the church's side entrance and Jeb followed her, his mind still on the problem revealed in his chart.

"You have a teenage daughter, Megan?"

"Yes." She hesitated but did not look at him. "Why?"

"I was thinking maybe we could start some sort of a youth program—like a café where the kids could come hang out after school and on weekends. Stay out of trouble and away from boredom and temptations."

"Sounds like a good idea. But I should warn you that Faith and most of her friends are at the stage where they just find adults' ideas antiquated and quaint."

"Actually, Mrs. Treadwell suggested asking you. Might you have some time to help me get the youth café going?"

"Me?" Her laughter was hollow and without real humor. "Oh, Reverend Matthews, there are so many people in the congregation who…"

"You know, Megan, you and I are neighbors and I hope we'll be friends, so do you think you might call me Jeb?"

"Reverend Dunhill preferred…"

"I'm not Reverend Dunhill, Megan—not by a long shot."

"Very well. Jeb it is, except when my daughter or other young people are around. Respect is important for them to learn."

"Good point. You know, I'm serious about needing help getting this project off the ground."

"I'm sure you are, but…"

"Just think about it, okay?" He took her arm and walked her to the door. "And please thank Mrs. Tread-well for the dinner invitation."

* * *

Megan started back toward the inn, but then she changed her mind and instead took the path that led her into the woods behind the church. As a child she had often hiked these woods when she needed to work through a problem—and she'd had more than her share. Whether to help with a youth group was pretty small potatoes compared to some of the things she'd had to deal with in her life. Yet, life being the circle that it was, eventually everything a person had ever done or not tied in with seemingly insignificant decisions.

There were two things that Megan understood about small towns and the people who lived in them. One, if you lived in a town long enough, made a good faith effort to clean up any mess you'd made, worked hard and went to church, past transgressions would eventually be forgiven. Two, when someone new came to town—someone like Jeb Matthews who was likely to stay awhile—that past could double back on you. The folks in Singing Springs were good people, but she knew that sooner or later Jeb would hear her story. And when he did, she wanted to be there to see his reaction. Maybe it was best that he heard it from her.

She turned and looked down on the church, then out toward the lake, the centerpiece of this town she'd called home for all of her thirty-two years. With a sigh of resignation, she squared her shoulders and retraced her steps.

He was still in his study considering the pie chart he'd made of the congregation.

"Reverend, I have something to tell you."

His eyes widened in surprise as he stood up and removed his reading glasses. "Has something happened?"

"Yes, but it was some time ago. Still, you need to

know. You'll hear soon enough, and frankly I'd just as soon you hear it from me—or maybe Reba, but I'm here now so..." She paused for breath. This was not going at all the way she had imagined.

"Megan, please, just sit down and start at the beginning."

She forced herself to take a deep breath and release it slowly. "As you know I have a daughter."

"Faith," he said.

"Yes. She's a good kid. No, she's an exceptional kid, and none of what happened is in any way her fault."

"Is Faith in some kind of trouble, Megan?"

She took a moment to answer. "No. I was the one in trouble. You see, when I was about Faith's age, I was dating a boy and, well, I got pregnant."

She wasn't sure what she had expected—disappointment, condemnation—anything but the concern and sympathy filling those soft green eyes. Somehow it made continuing her story that much more difficult.

"Danny denied that the baby was his, although he knew I'd never been with another boy. I'd only been with him, the one time."

Jeb frowned. "But this young man refused responsibility?"

"He was very popular, captain of the football team, and he was off to college the following month on a full scholarship. Becoming a father would have changed everything for him. His dad was on the town council and an elder in the church. His mother was the school guidance counselor."

"Still, he must have known..."

He wasn't getting this. How could he? There was a chasm in lifestyle between people brought up in the small towns of the north woods and those raised in the cities and suburbs. From everything Reba had told her about Jeb Matthews, he'd spent most of his adult life in Chicago managing a global company and chairing society events that raised huge sums of money for charity. What possible frame of reference did he have for a small-town girl who'd gotten herself pregnant at sixteen?

She decided to give him the brunt of the story. "Danny knew but, as he said, who would take the word of a girl whose mother abandoned her when she was eight and whose father was the town drunk? He had a point." She waited for the inevitable response—pity, shock and then just the slightest narrowing of the eyes to show a change of opinion about her.

Jeb's eyes remained wide-open and steady. "I'm so sorry, Megan. Still, there must have been someone in town who saw through his lie. Someone must have known you were telling the truth."

"Lots of people probably knew, but only Reba stood up for me. After Faith was born, she took us in and we've been together ever since." She sucked in a deep breath. "The point of telling you this is so that you'll understand why I'm not the go-to person in this town when it comes to organizing anything—especially for young people. I'm not exactly Singing Springs's idea of a role model."

He shook his head. "I'm afraid I don't get the connection."

"What I'm trying to say is that you'll have a lot more success organizing this youth project if you pull some of the other parents into it."

"Well, sure. Actually, the whole idea is to get the kids interested in coming to things at the church, and then hopefully the parents will follow. This segment—" he pointed to his pie chart where a thin slice represented Megan's age group "—will look more like this larger slice representing the over-fifty group."

She was relieved that he'd turned his attention back to the youth group and away from her past. "Take my advice, Jeb, and think of me as more of a worker bee. I'm happy to help you in any support role you might need—setting up, organizing the food, that sort of thing."

"I'm sure you could do that kind of thing with one hand tied behind your back. Reba tells me you're the queen of multitasking and coordinating. She says that you're practically running the inn these days."

"She exaggerates."

He shrugged. "Maybe, but she doesn't strike me as someone who would willingly turn over responsibility for her livelihood to just anyone."

So that was it. This all had to be Reba's idea. Her friend and employer had sent her here instead of simply calling Jeb herself to invite him for supper and give him the afghan. She and Jeb had spoken about this and Reba must have hinted that Megan would be good at anything involving young people.

So he hadn't been distracted from her past after all. "Reba and I are more than employer and employee. She's been like a mother to me and she wants the best for me. It's just that sometimes her ideas about what's best and mine don't jibe."

"For example?"

"As soon as Faith started school, Reba began her campaign for me to go back to school at night and on weekends."

"Sounds like a good idea."

"I took a few courses, but my first priority will

always be my daughter. Faith is my reason for getting up every morning. I am determined to give her the very best chance she can have at being happy and successful in life, and nothing comes ahead of that."

Jeb looked down at his folded hands for a long moment as if lost in thought. When he looked up again, the light of excitement she'd seen in his eyes when he'd talked about the youth project was gone. In its place was an expression of such sadness and pain that she placed her hand on his forearm. Did this youth café mean that much to him?

"Hey, there are plenty of people in the congregation who would be more than willing to help you get this idea off the ground. People others would be more than willing to follow. It's really a great idea, Jeb."

He smiled. "I'm not going to give up on you, Megan. In business my employees used to call me bullheaded—among other things and always behind my back, of course."

She couldn't help smiling.

"Hey, how about a compromise? I won't openly involve you—yet—and you agree to think about the youth project and how you would set it up if you were going to take charge. Then you and I can talk about your ideas. Nobody else has to know you're even on the team if that's what you want."

"Why is having me involved in this so important to you?"

He looked a little taken aback at the question. "The truth?"

She nodded.

"Truth is I don't know exactly, but my whole life I've gone with my instincts and there's something about you, Megan Osbourne. Reba may have called my attention to you, but after hearing your story, I have an even stronger feeling that you're going to be a key to my success here."

She saw his statement for the compliment it was and blushed. There had been a time when people in town had expected big things of her. "You know, when I was Faith's age—I mean before…Danny—folks around here looked at me as the kid who could overcome the worst possible family situation and still make something of herself. But all that changed once I became pregnant. I had disappointed them, spoiled their hopes for my future."

"That was on them, Megan. Not you. I doubt you asked for the responsibility to make something of yourself just so others could feel pride. And it doesn't mean you haven't succeeded over the course of your life so far. It just means you deviated from the path that others set for you."

It had been so long since she'd thought of herself as anything more than Faith's mother and Reba's helper. To have this virtual stranger see beyond that was unsettling, to say the least. "I should go," she said, glancing at the clock above his desk. "Reba will wonder how long it takes to deliver an extra blanket." She smiled and held out her hand. "Thanks for listening and understanding."

For the second time that afternoon they shook hands, but this time he prolonged the grasp. "Think about it, Megan. What better way to do something for your daughter than to help me get this youth café going?"

He had a point. Lately Faith had been mooning around about a boy whose family had been spending summers in Singing Springs for several years. At the end of the previous summer Caleb Armstrong had shown an interest in Faith. He reminded Megan a lot of Danny Moreland, and she was bound and determined that no boy would break her daughter's heart the way Danny had broken hers.

"Okay, you win," she said. "But I am strictly a behind-the-scenes person."

"Understood." He gave her a sharp salute. "Thanks."

As she walked quickly across the churchyard and down to the inn, she had trouble containing her smile and her suddenly light heart. Was it possible that Jeb was right? That the two of them might do something that would help Faith and all the youth in Singing Springs?

But her high spirits plummeted like a kite abruptly bereft of wind when she entered the inn and heard Nellie Barnsworth lecturing Reba. The two women were standing on the inn's expansive front porch, unaware that Megan had come in through the kitchen.

"Now, Reba, we're all aware that you've set your sights on finding a proper husband for Megan. If it weren't so shocking it would be laughable for you to think for one moment that Megan, with her personal and family history, and a man of the cloth could ever…"

"Hold your horses, Nellie," Reba interrupted. "I would remind you that Jeb is our neighbor as well as our pastor. No one is trying to force anything here."

Megan heard Nellie snort. "You don't fool me, Reba. I'm warning you to back off before that poor girl is hurt yet again."

That poor girl… How often over the course of her life had she heard that when people thought she wasn't around? Still, Nellie had a point. Any association between her and the minister, regardless of how innocent, was bound to raise questions, concerns and eyebrows. This time she had to agree with Nellie.

The hard part was going to be getting Reba to back off now that Nellie had challenged her.

Chapter Two

It rained for most of the rest of the week and Faith got the flu, so it was fairly easy for Megan to keep her distance from Jeb. She even stayed away from church services, saying she needed to be sure Faith was all right. But Reba had not given up, and on Thursday when the sun finally broke through Megan heard the front door of the inn slam as the older woman's heavy footsteps came down the hall. At age seventy-two Reba often suffered from crippling arthritis, especially in her hip. It was one of the reasons that Megan had taken on even more of the responsibility for running the inn.

"Megan! We have a guest!"

It was early in the season for anyone to visit the inn, but Megan knew that tone. She planted a smile on her face and prepared to greet the new arrival. Still, her smile froze when she realized Reba's guest was none other than Jeb Matthews.

"Reverend Matthews will be staying with us beginning tonight," Reba announced in the same no-nonsense way she handled most communication. With Reba's squat frame blocking the doorway, Jeb grinned at Megan.

Megan forced herself to pay attention to what Reba was saying. "I told Henry Epstein that basement wall was bowed," Reba huffed. "But would he listen? No. Had to wait for the rains to prove me right, and now here you are with a basement full of water and the roof falling in and…"

Reba paused midsentence, as was her habit when she was on one of her rants. She took a long breath, flicked her eyes toward the ceiling, seeking forgiveness, and continued in a calmer tone. "But no matter. I'm just glad we have the room—another month and we might be fully booked but May is quieter and…"

Jeb eased past Reba. "What is that you're baking, Megan? It smells wonderful."

"It's cinnamon rolls," she said. "They'll be ready soon. Would you like one?"

"Well, of course, he wants one, Meggie. Look at the man. Hasn't had a decent meal since he got here, running around trying to meet with everyone."

"They fed me," Jeb said.

"Rubber chicken. Time you had a good square meal, and now that you'll be staying here you can just figure to take your meals with Megan, Faith and me."

"Actually, Mrs. Barnsworth mentioned she was going to bring over a casserole later. Perhaps…"

"I'll just bet she did," Reba muttered, glancing at Megan. "You may as well know now, Reverend, Nellie Barnsworth sees people and events through a unique set of glasses, and unfortunately they aren't usually rose-colored. Take everything she tells you with several grains of salt."

Aware that Reba was on the verge of explaining how

Megan and Faith had come to live with her, Megan found her courage and her tongue. "Jeb knows all about what happened with Danny, Reba. I told him myself."

Reba's eyebrows shot up in surprise and then she smiled. "Well, good for you, child." She turned her attention back to Jeb. "Now, let's get you settled while I call Nellie and let her know that a casserole will be most appreciated."

"There's also the matter of rent," Jeb said, reaching for his wallet.

For a moment Megan actually felt a little sorry for the guy. She knew Reba well enough to understand that she intended to give him the room and that she did not take kindly to her gifts being rejected. She sidled behind Reba and tried to signal him to drop the subject.

"I see you back there, missy," Reba said.

"Always said you had eyes in the back of your head," Megan replied, remembering the older woman catching her at forbidden actions when she was a child.

"In the back, on top and on either side," Reba retorted. "Now then, Jeb, you're new at this ministry thing as well as at living in a small town. You lived in Chicago, I believe, before coming here?"

"Yes, ma'am." He looked over at Megan for help, but the timer chimed and Megan turned away to check on the rolls.

"Well, I don't know how they do neighborly things in the city—I never set foot in any town larger than Eagle River. But here if a neighbor offers you something there is no price tag attached. You get my meaning?"

Megan set the metal baking tray on the counter with a clatter as she glanced up to see how Jeb was taking this.

"But this place is your livelihood, and it could be

several weeks before we can get the parsonage inhabitable again and…"

Reba's long-suffering sigh cut him off. "All right. We'll compromise. You don't pay rent, but you lend a hand with the chores. There's lots to do to get a place as old as this one ready for the season. Flower beds that will need cleaning out and replanting, for instance."

"I'm a little out of practice, but I'm sure it will come back to me. I grew up on a farm, after all."

"Really? I never would have guessed." Reba grinned. "Well, now, Megan, how fortunate for us is that?"

"So I'll help with the chores and, to show my appreciation for you ladies rescuing me in my hour of need, how about I take the two of you out for dinner once a week?"

"The three of us," Reba corrected. "Our little Faith comes with the package."

Megan was surprised to see the same inexplicable cloud of sadness pass over the minister's features that she'd noticed that day in his study. She was sure there must be a connection, but couldn't imagine what it might be. In any case, he recovered quickly and extended his hand to Reba. "Deal."

"Deal," she agreed. "Right, Megan?" She jerked her head, indicating that Megan should shake Jeb's hand, as well.

"Deal," she murmured, giving his hand a quick but firm grasp.

"Good. Now how about pointing the way to my quarters so I can get settled in?"

Reba pulled a key from a row of hooks by the back door and handed it to Megan. "Number one," she said and winked. When Megan had been in her twenties, Reba had often had several candidates for Megan.

"Number one" had always been her way of saying, "He's at the top of the list." Of course, none had worked out and, after one turned out to be married, she'd backed off. Megan had been relieved because she'd realized that Reba wasn't much better than Megan at judging men other than her own late and beloved Stan.

"This way." Megan led the pastor down a narrow hall to a suite with its own private entrance and a view of the lake. It was the best room in the inn, which was exactly why Reba had dubbed it the honeymoon suite.

"Wow," Jeb said as he stepped inside and headed straight for the large window that overlooked the lake. "This is really terrific."

Megan watched as he explored the nooks and crannies of the suite, opening the closet, checking out the desk. Then suddenly shy at being alone with him again, she busied herself making sure the small refrigerator in the kitchenette was stocked. When she turned around Jeb was looking at the bed and frowning.

Megan immediately understood why. Reba's romantic side had been firmly in control when she'd decorated this room. The bed was festooned with pillows in all sizes and shapes—including heart-shaped ones—and a canopy of lace was swagged and draped above the perimeter of the large antique bed.

"Uh, I'm six-two and, well…" Jeb scratched his head as he studied the length of the bed.

"It's the pillows," Megan said, as she hurried to remove all of them except the regular bed pillows. She opened a cedar chest at the foot of the bed, pushed aside extra blankets and jammed the pillows inside. "See?"

"Better," he agreed, but he kept casting his eyes toward the lace canopy.

"And that canopy cloth needs a good laundering anyway," Megan said as she started dismantling the lace panels from the artificial rose vine that Reba had used to hold them in place. "I'll just take it down and then once you move back to the parsonage I'll put it back. No big deal."

She was babbling nervously. This was beyond ridiculous. How many guests—male guests—had she helped get settled into their rooms over the years? Some of them had even made passes at her and she'd had to bite her lip to keep from losing her professional cool and putting them in their place. Jeb was barely looking at her, much less making a pass, as he reached up and unhooked the lace from a post.

"You're sure Reba won't mind?"

"Not a bit. I'm sure she chose this room for you because it's the only one with its own entrance, and it has the desk and the view of the lake."

"Inspiration?" There was that smile again.

"Divine inspiration," Megan said automatically, and then gasped as she realized she had just corrected a minister, a man with a doctorate of divinity. "Sorry."

"For what? You're right, you know. Only God could have created something like that view."

Megan bundled the yards of lace into a ball. "Still, to someone like you—I mean, you probably automatically assume that God…" *Oh, somebody shut me up now,* she thought.

Jeb frowned. "You know, Megan, that's the one thing about being a minister that's going to take some getting used to. The idea that people think I must naturally have God on my mind 24/7."

"Don't you?"

"I'm just another of God's creatures—get it? Creatures? Creations? I'm no more tuned in than you are, or Reba or Faith for that matter."

Megan relaxed slightly. The one thing in her life that gave her personal satisfaction was the way Faith had turned out, in spite of everything they had gone through together. "Faith is truly God's child," she said softly, then she smiled. "She doesn't fully realize that yet."

"Anxious to find her own way. That's pretty typical."

"I suppose."

"She'll do it," he said. "You did, and I suspect that growing up with two strong women like you and Reba, Faith has a better than average chance of making her way in this world."

"That's very kind of you."

"No," he said, and his tone was so fierce that Megan gave him her full attention. "You—and Reba—have been there every day, through everything," he said. "That's so important for a child."

Megan wasn't sure what response he expected, so she just nodded and waited for the rest of the sermon.

"Hey, sorry about that," Jeb said. "Coming down out of my pulpit now."

"Do you need some help moving the rest of your things down? I could have Faith…"

"That's okay. I'll take care of it." He glanced at his watch. "I've been asked to give the blessing at the Chamber of Commerce luncheon today. After that I'll stop by the parsonage and load up my car. See you later?"

Megan nodded and handed him the keys to his room. "Welcome to the Cranberry Hill Inn," she said as she would have with any guest. "If there's anything we can do to make your stay more pleasant…"

Jeb grinned. "Two things. Save me one of those

cinnamon rolls and help me get that youth café up and running."

Megan couldn't help laughing. "Your employees were right, you know. You don't give up, do you?"

"Nope, but keep in mind that you offered—anything to make my stay more pleasant."

"I might have a couple of ideas," she said.

"Knew you would." He gave her that self-assured grin that had single women all over town comparing him to their favorite film or television star.

"We'll talk," she promised. "Later. You're going to be late for the Chamber meeting."

He glanced at his watch and ran a hand through his hair as he grabbed his sport coat and headed out the open door. "Later," he called.

"Hey, Pastor Matthews," Henry Epstein shouted that afternoon when Jeb stopped by the parsonage to pack. Henry and his son, Rick, were stretching blue tarps to prevent more rain from seeping through the exposed rafters. "Better pray those storm clouds over there aren't headed this way. Last thing you need right now is more rain."

"We'll leave the weather up to the good Lord, Henry. He has His reasons."

Henry removed his battered baseball cap and scratched his bald head. "Well, forgive me for saying so, Pastor, but maybe God has other things on His mind and has failed to notice your problem here."

Jeb laughed. "It'll all work out, Henry. You'll see. Let me know when the supplies are delivered and I'll give you a hand."

"Tomorrow," Henry called back and then turned his attention back to the task at hand.

Jeb spotted Megan setting up food and lemonade on the warped picnic table that sat on one side of the house. "Henry? Reba sent you and Rick a snack," she shouted.

"Leave it," Henry shouted back. "We need to finish this before those clouds open up."

"That's quite a spread," Jeb said, crossing the yard.

"There's plenty here," she agreed. "I'm sure the guys wouldn't mind if you joined them."

"Looks like that might be a while. Okay if I have something now? I got to talking to folks at the Chamber and never got lunch." He sat down on one side of the picnic table and indicated a place for her.

"Swiss or cheddar?" Megan offered.

"How about some of each?" Jeb separated a paper plate from the stack and held it out to her as she un-wrapped the cheeses and a package of crackers. She then opened a bag of chips and a container of carrot and celery sticks and offered each to Jeb.

Jeb filled two cups with lemonade from the thermos. "It seems like I've been here forever and at the same time like I just arrived."

"You're doing fine," she assured him. "After all, this is all new to you. You didn't even seem nervous that first Sunday."

He leaned closer and whispered, "Truth? I was ter-rified."

Megan laughed.

"You think I'm kidding? My knees were shaking so much that I was sure those people in the front pews could hear them knocking together. I imagined someone saying, 'What's that clicking sound?' just when I reached the high point of my sermon."

"It was a good sermon," Megan said. "So different

from Reverend Dunhill. Somehow I always left his sermons feeling as if I hadn't done right by God all week long."

"And how did you feel after my service?" Jeb couldn't resist asking.

"Are you fishing for compliments, Pastor?" she teased.

"Yep. Fire away."

Her smile faded. "Hopeful," she said quietly. "Like no matter how bad things might seem for someone, God would be there."

"That's what I was going for," Jeb said.

"On the other hand, you have your work cut out for you. Pastor Dunhill was an institution in this town."

"I'm hoping I can show folks a different style of ministry, something a little more open. Something that will have them stop making comparisons."

"Well, now there is that curiosity factor to be considered, not to mention the single-guy factor—no disrespect to your profession. Together they might buy you some time. No offense."

"None taken." They ate in comfortable silence for several seconds and then Jeb said, "I was married, you know. My wife died a few years ago."

"I'm so sorry." Megan resisted the instinct to reach across the table and touch his hand.

"Thanks," Jeb said, his voice husky. He stood up and started to gather up the trash. "Well, I've got some packing to do and a sermon to write. I'll see you at supper?"

"Sure. I…"

But Jeb was already heading for the house, his long strides covering the distance quickly and the snap of the screen door punctuating his quick exit.

Chapter Three

Megan sat at the table for several minutes, staring up at the parsonage without really seeing it. Instead she was thinking about assumptions she and others were guilty of making about those who had chosen the ministry as their life's work. As a child she had believed that Reverend Dunhill had a direct line to God. As a pregnant teen, she had sought his counsel and been disappointed to realize that he, like others in town, believed she had brought her misfortune on herself. He had advised her to pray and mend her ways. And as a young mother, she had attended services to please Reba more than because church was a place where she could find spiritual comfort.

Had it ever occurred to her that maybe Reverend Dunhill had had his own problems—troubles and regrets that colored the way he brought God's word to the congregation? Maybe he had suffered a tragic loss in his life or, like her, had always had misgivings and doubts about his ability to meet the challenges God had set before him. Either way, Reverend Dunhill had always been another authority figure to Megan. But Jeb Matthews was different. There was something about him that made her want to trust him and at the same time befriend him.

"It's because he's much closer in age to you," she muttered to herself. "Reverend Dunhill was more of a father figure, or grandfather. Jeb is like a contemporary and you can talk to him—one adult to another." She watched him load a box of books into his car, then return to the parsonage for more of his things. Megan crossed the yard and knocked at the open back door of the parsonage.

"Hi," she said when Jeb answered the door, a duffel in one hand and a computer bag slung over his shoulder.

"Hi," he replied.

"I forgot to tell you that I've been giving some serious thought to your idea for a youth café. It's really a great idea. Small towns have their advantages, but offering enough opportunities for young people to get together in an atmosphere that's fun but safe isn't one of them." She was babbling again and paused to take a long, steadying breath. "It occurs to me that Faith has a wide circle of friends and she's great at getting them to do things. Maybe they could paint the church basement, brighten the place up."

His smile was like a flag unfurling on a breezy spring wind. "That would be great, Megan. Just terrific. Thank you."

"No problem," Megan replied, sounding more like teenaged Faith than someone capable of putting together a successful youth project. On top of that, her feet felt as if they'd suddenly sunk into concrete. She couldn't seem to move. "Well, I should be getting back."

"I'll give you a ride. I'm all done here." He rolled the

duffel onto the porch and handed her the computer bag.
"If you can handle this, I'll get the rest."

Megan hooked the bag over her shoulder while Jeb
stepped back inside the house and returned carrying a
large box stacked with books. "Let me just load this stuff
in the trunk and we're set."

"I can walk," she said. "I mean, it's just down the hill,
and you might need the space."

"Nope." He hoisted the heavy box onto the backseat
of his car, put the duffel in the trunk and then relieved
her of the computer bag, setting it in the trunk, as well.
"Traveling light," he said with a grin as he closed the
trunk and headed for the passenger side.

When she realized he was opening the door for her,
Megan blushed. It had been some time since a man had
shown her that courtesy. "Thanks," she murmured.

"You know what?" he asked when he got behind the
wheel of the hybrid and started the quiet motor. "I
haven't had time to really see the whole community the
chapel serves. Seems to me that as a native you'd be the
perfect guide for the nickel tour of Singing Springs.
That is, if you have some time."

"Right now?"

"No time like the present, as my mother always says.
It won't take long."

Megan could not help laughing. "That's for sure."
The commercial district of Singing Springs ran from the
inn at one end of town to the post office and town hall
three blocks north. "Okay, sure."

It was only when she saw Nellie Barnsworth coming
out of the Cut and Dry Beauty Shop on Main Street that
she realized her mistake. Driving through town with
the new minister would certainly start tongues wagging,

and no tongue wagged faster than Nellie's. When Jeb raised his hand in greeting and Nellie responded with a weak smile and then hurried back inside the beauty shop, Megan didn't need a vivid imagination to guess the conversation inside those walls.

But instead of slinking lower in the seat as she might have years earlier, Megan sat up a little straighter and smiled as she pointed out landmarks to Jeb. "Teresa Samuels owns the beauty shop there. Her husband, Charley, has the gas station in the next block. There's the bank, of course. Fred Barnsworth is the bank president, but then since he's also president of the board at the church, you must know that."

"Good man," Jeb said. "So far everyone you've mentioned is a member of the church."

"Well, yeah, most people here attend church—maybe not your church but…"

He chuckled. "It's hardly my church, Megan. At least I hope that's not how people see it."

"Figure of speech," Megan said softly and fought against the familiar sense of inadequacy. One thing from her past that she had failed to overcome was the way she was intimidated by anyone with a college education. And Jeb—well, he had his Ph.D.

They rode the next block in silence. "What's the Shack?" he asked as they passed a sprawling old building painted in vivid red, white and blue.

"It's sort of a general store for tourists. There's a soda fountain and ice cream shop at that far end, and then at the other they stock fishing equipment and live bait and water toys for the kids. And in the middle is Jessica's Northwoods Boutique. T-shirts and sweatshirts mostly," Megan added when Jeb glanced over.

"And is there a Jessica?"

"Oh, sure. Jessica and Pete Burbank. She handles the boutique while Pete handles the tackle and bait shop."

"And who serves up the ice cream?"

"They have four kids—twin boys age twelve and the two girls. Maria is the youngest at ten, and Cindy is two years younger than Faith. They all help out in whatever way they can."

"Sounds like we could have a good start on the café if we just get Faith and half the Burbank kids to show up." He pulled into a parking space. "How about some ice cream? I'd like to meet the family if that's okay with you?"

"Sure." What was she going to say? That Jessica Burbank had once been her best friend? That Jessica's brother, Danny, was the one who had impregnated her and then denied it? That even after college when Jessica returned to Singing Springs and married Pete, her high school sweetheart, she had maintained only a polite but distant relationship with Megan? And that Danny, now married and living out west somewhere, had told his lie so many times that he'd come to believe it himself?

"Sure," she said again and reached for the door handle.

"Megan?"

She opened the car door, but remained seated and did not turn at the sound of her name, too afraid of what her face might reveal.

"We can do this another time if you'd rather. I mean, if there's some reason you…"

Megan closed the door and refastened her seat belt. "You know that business I told you the other day about my past? Well, there's a little more to it. How about we take a drive around the lake and you tell me what Nellie

Barnsworth and others might have told you about me, and I'll fill in the blanks?"

To her surprise, Jeb seemed to instinctively understand that something had triggered her sudden change of mood. Without comment he drove until they reached the turn onto the road that circled the lake. After a minute he pointed to a sign indicating a trail next to a small parking lot. "Would it be okay if we walked a little way on the nature trail? It's such a mild day and you know how spring goes in the Midwest—one day spring and the next back to winter. I like to take advantage of these days when they come."

"Okay." Megan was already having second thoughts. She should have just agreed to the ice cream. The truth was that she'd panicked at the idea of encountering Jessica Burbank in the new minister's company. Not that Jessica would do or say anything inappropriate. She and Megan might no longer be friends, but Jessica was still a woman that Megan admired and respected.

She realized the car had stopped and she and Jeb were just sitting there. "The trail might be really boggy," she said, as if that topic had been uppermost on her mind.

"If it gets too wet we can always turn back." He turned slightly so that she knew he was looking directly at her. "You have to make a start, Megan, before you know for sure."

They were no longer talking about the trail.

Megan sighed and opened her car door and Jeb followed suit. "What has Nellie Barnsworth told you about me?" she asked as they approached a sign mapping out the trail choices.

Jeb selected a knobby branch from those left by previous hikers and handed it to her. "In case the muck starts to win," he said and took the second staff for himself. "And I'm not going to repeat what anyone tells me, Megan—about you or someone else. You tell me as much as you want me to know and we'll leave it at that." He indicated that she should lead the way. "It's your story, Megan, not theirs."

She opened her mouth, closed it, then tried to start again. How to frame it so that—what? He thought well of her? He pitied her? He was angry at Danny Moreland for not taking responsibility for getting her pregnant? What did she want from him?

"Just say it, Megan," he said gently, "or don't. It's your choice. But know this—whatever you tell me today will not be repeated, and I am not interested in judging you. It's just that you seemed so troubled when I mentioned going inside that store." She heard him chuckle. "In my business, at least the one I'm in these days, that triggers a response."

"What kind of response?" Good, let him keep talking and she wouldn't need to say much.

"While I was in divinity school, I became interested in words and their meaning. I guess I wanted to be especially careful that whatever words I use to deliver a sermon were the correct words, ones that couldn't be misunderstood."

Megan felt herself relax as she picked her way over rocks and tree roots along the path that skimmed the lake's shore. "Such as?"

"Minister," he said. "Think about it. A minister is one who ministers, but what does that mean really? Well, I discovered that if you go through several layers of synonyms it can mean many things—to nurture, support, serve, sustain and even to befriend. Although

that takes matters to a higher level involving things like trust, confidence, faith."

Megan did what she always seemed to do in circumstances where she was mistaken for someone far more educated and sophisticated than she was. She put herself down.

"I never thought of it like that." She glanced back at him, took a deep breath and plunged into the icy waters of her past. "As you know, I got pregnant in the fall of my senior year. I graduated, but that was the end of formal schooling for me. Not that I would have gone on to college anyway. We didn't have the money." *Because Dad had no job and drank up whatever we had coming in from the county.*

Megan set her jaw and started up the path that wound to the top of a bluff. After the thunder of her humiliation died, she heard Jeb coming behind her. At the top of the rise he caught up with her and touched her shoulder. She paused but did not turn.

"You know what I figured out, about the time I decided to apply for divinity school?"

She shook her head, afraid to trust her voice.

"Real education comes with living in the real world. Oh, book learning certainly has its place. For one thing it broadens our worldview and can give us tools for understanding how the world works—how God intended for His world to be. But it's how we meet the challenges that come our way in life that provides the greatest lessons."

"Thank you," she murmured, knowing that his words were meant to console and heal.

"Let's sit for a minute," he suggested, indicating a weathered wooden bench overlooking the lake. The inn and church were visible on the far side.

Megan sat, but kept her focus on that distant shore.

"What's the connection with the Burbanks, Megan?"

"Faith's father is Jessica Burbank's brother."

"Danny?"

"Yeah. He started denying it, and pretty soon every-one believed him. He even believed it."

"He still has no part in Faith's life?" Megan could not help noticing that Jeb's voice had tightened, and she glanced up at him.

"It's hard to blame him, really. We were teenagers and he had this full scholarship to play football at a college in California. It had been his dream since I could remember. Eventually he married and had a short career as a professional ballplayer and then became a sports-caster for a television station out there. He built a career, had a real family…."

"You and Faith were a real family," Jeb snapped. "Sorry, sometimes I lose the objectivity. A work in progress," he added.

His very real and human reaction to the choices Danny had made gave Megan the confidence she needed to continue. "Trust me, I wasn't always so understanding. When he denied being with me, knowing he was my first and only…" She blushed. "You know," she mumbled.

"But in time you forgave him?"

She shrugged. "Sometimes the people you trust most in life can disappoint you. They might even leave you and never look back. I've known that since I was eight and my mother left my dad and me. Reba helped me understand that wasn't my fault, and when Faith was little and asked about her father, I tried to teach her the same lesson."

"And now?"

"She never asks about him."

"She knows who he is?"

Megan looked at him and smiled. "She knows who Reba and I say he is, and she knows who the rest of Singing Springs believes he was—a summer visitor who swept me off my feet and then left town."

"And which version does Faith believe?"

Megan shrugged. "Hard to say. She doesn't talk about it at all. She did when she was younger, but I suspect it's become easier to buy into the second version."

"And that's all right with you?"

"Here's what life has taught me, Jeb. The will to survive is a powerful and even intoxicating thing. If the challenges are great enough you'll accept what you need to to come through it as unscathed as possible." She saw his eyes widen slightly. She assumed that he was surprised to hear such a complex thought come out of someone like her.

"And Jessica?"

"Jessica was my best friend even though she was two years older. We just clicked. She was away at college when I realized I was pregnant. I can't blame her for believing her brother."

"But when she came back here to live?"

"By that time we were different people. Not much had turned out the way either of us had dreamed when we were kids. She had her family and a business to run. It wasn't like we were mad at each other or anything. I understood that family ties were more powerful—I respected that. I guess I had always envied that a little," she said, more to herself than to him. She stood up. "We should head back."

Jeb followed her back down the trail, along the shore and out to the car without registering anything beyond the line of Megan's shoulders and head held tall and proud. He held the car door for her. She smiled and murmured a thank-you as she ducked inside.

He got in, started the engine and then sat there for a long moment. "You know, Megan, that part about one of the synonyms for *minister* being *to befriend?*"

Her nod was almost imperceptible and she looked at her hands folded in her lap.

"Well, I'd like us to be friends if that's all right with you. One thing I've noticed about Singing Springs is the absence of a lot of people in my age group—folks are either a lot older or a lot younger. I imagine it can get pretty lonely."

"I don't want pity," she said through lips drawn tight.

"Who said anything about pity? The truth is I could use a friend. I may be the new preacher in town and already I understand that the position carries a lot of weight with the local population. But it can be pretty lonely standing up there behind that pulpit by myself, looking out at pews filled with expectant faces."

"Why me?"

"I'm not sure," he admitted. "Maybe it was the way you trusted me back there. Maybe I'm just trying to get on your good side so I don't miss out on those cinnamon rolls for breakfast."

He saw the smallest twitch of her lips—a twitch that could lead to a smile.

"Then it's Reba you want to befriend. She sets up the menus. I just do the baking."

"I see." But he didn't see at all. He wanted to ask why she put herself down that way, why baking wasn't at least as great a contribution as making up the menu, but her trust seemed too fragile to challenge. "Well, as a friend, maybe you could put in a good word for me?"

The smile blossomed. "I could, but the truth is if we don't get back soon Reba's likely to send out a search and rescue party." She finally glanced his way. "Drive," she said.

Jeb grinned and shifted the car into gear.

They were mostly silent on the ride back to the inn. She pointed out a couple of additional landmarks. He expressed polite interest. And then they were turning onto the drive at the inn. He pulled the car around to the side entrance near his room. "Thanks again for the tour, Megan."

She had gotten out of the car, but had not yet started inside. "There's one more thing you need to know," she said.

He'd been lifting the box of books from the trunk, but he gave her his full attention. Something in her tone told him whatever was coming was important.

"My dad?"

"Yeah?"

"He started drinking when my mother left. Eventually he lost his job and we had to take welfare from the county."

"Does he still live here?"

"After Faith and I moved in with Reba, he left town and sent word that he'd checked himself into the VA hospital in Milwaukee."

"If you like, I'll go with you when you visit," Jeb offered.

"He left there shortly after that. No forwarding address—just gone." She fanned the fingers of one hand like a magician doing a card trick. "Reba and Faith are my family, Jeb. They've been the only real family I've ever known. Everybody else chose to leave."

She started for the side door.

"Megan?"

But she was already inside.

What would he have told her? That no one could choose their family—only their friends? That she wasn't responsible for her father's fall into alcohol any more than she was for Faith's father abandoning them? That people you loved could be there one day and gone the next?

"She knows all that," he muttered as he carried his belongings into the room he would call home for the next few weeks. "As her pastor, surely you can come up with something more than the platitudes she's probably heard her whole life." But it was times like this when Jeb felt inadequate to serve as anyone's minister.

Chapter Four

Megan could not believe that in less than an hour she had given Jeb Matthews the digest version of her life story. She barely knew the man.

"Well, it's done," she muttered to herself as she hefted a load of wet linens from the washer to the dryer. "At least this way he heard it from me and not…"

"Who on earth are you talking to?" Reba asked, crowding her way into the narrow laundry room with a basket stacked high with towels.

"Me, myself and I," Megan replied, relieving Reba of her heavy burden. "What are you doing hauling this around when you know very well the doctor told you no heavy lifting with that hip of yours?"

"My, my, we're in a good mood." Reba studied her closely. "Something you want to talk about?"

"No. I mean, I'm fine. Nothing wrong."

"Uh-huh," Reba said, clearly unconvinced. "Saw you and the preacher come back a while ago—together." When Megan said nothing, Reba waited a beat, then added, "Have a nice lunch, did you?"

"We did. Henry and Rick told me to be sure and thank you."

Reba snorted. "I'm not asking about the Epsteins and you know it, missy. Now, what happened?"

"Oh, the minister?" Megan lifted her eyebrows as if just catching on to Reba's true interest. Then she grinned. "We had lunch, then he offered me a ride back down the hill since he was coming this way."

Reba looked pointedly at the old kitchen clock she kept on the wall in the laundry room. "Must have either been quite a leisurely lunch or else you took quite a detour. It's no more than a five-minute trip from the parsonage down to here."

"He asked for a tour of the town." Megan shrugged.

"Another sixteen minutes tops," Reba muttered.

"We drove by the lake and stopped at the nature trail. That view looking back at town from the rise there is so picturesque."

"And was this a silent retreat or did the two of you actually converse?"

"Reba, this isn't like you. Nellie Barnsworth will dig and pick until she gets every last morsel about an encounter that interests her. Not you. What gives?"

"You're upset. You were with the preacher. I want to know if there's a connection. The man seems like the real deal and I'd like to think he'll be a fine replacement for Reverend Dunhill, but he's still on probation as far as I'm concerned." Reba eased herself into the wicker chair and folded her arms over her chest. "Might as well tell me."

Megan pushed herself onto the top of the dryer, her feet dangling the way they had when she'd first started helping out at the inn as a child. "He wanted to stop in at the Shack and introduce himself."

"Ah," Reba said, and Megan knew that she had fully grasped the problem. "And did you?"

"No. I thought he needed to hear from me what happened and then he could meet Danny's sister."

"So you told him about Faith…"

"And about my mother leaving and Dad's drinking—oh, he got the whole picture."

The dryer's timer shrilled, but neither woman moved.

"Why do you do that, child?" Reba said wearily.

"Do what?"

"It's almost like you want to push people away. You've done it your whole life."

"I haven't. I don't," Megan protested, as she hopped off the dryer and began unloading it. "It's just that Jeb is— Well, as a minister and one who is new to this congregation, he's in a unique position when it comes to people telling him things, and I just thought…"

"You don't think. That's the problem. You react based on what you imagine people are going to do or say." Reba reached for a pillowcase and folded it, pressing the wrinkles out with flat hands. "I've told you this before, Megan—you are not your parents. They had their troubles and their challenges and met them the only way they knew how at the time. I expect they both carry around a lot of regrets. You, on the other hand, have no need to regret the decisions you've made or to put yourself down for how you've played the cards you were dealt. You've earned your place in this community and in the hearts and minds of those who live here. End of story."

Megan was well aware that whenever Reba uttered those three words, she meant them. For Reba this conversation had come to its natural conclusion. Change the topic, stay silent or leave the room, because for Reba there was nothing more to be said on the topic of Megan's confession to Jeb Matthews.

But Megan had plenty to think about—which was, of course, exactly what Reba intended.

On Sunday morning Jeb awoke with a start. He'd been dreaming about Deborah and Sally. Well, not exactly about them. The dream had been about his work—the work he'd done before. He needed to meet a deadline and then get home for something important. Deborah was going to be upset. His stockholders were going to be furious. He was headed straight for disaster and nothing he could do or say would avert it. Then the phone rang—in his dream and on the nightstand next to the canopied bed.

He shook off the familiar nightmare and reached for his phone, noting the digital clock read 5:47 a.m.

"Pastor?"

He tried to place the voice, male, unsteady, familiar. "Yes?"

"It's Rick Epstein, Henry's son. I'm really sorry to call so early, but it's Dad. He's had a heart attack. We're at the hospital and the doctor says it doesn't look good, and me and Mom were wondering…"

Jeb sat on the side of the bed, reaching for his clothes as he listened to Rick tell him how his father had seemed just fine, but then had gotten up in the middle of the night and collapsed. The paramedics had come right away and brought the older man to the hospital in Eagle River. "Tell your mom that I'm on my way," Jeb said.

"Thanks."

As soon as he'd dressed, Jeb headed out to the inn's kitchen, hoping to grab a banana or muffin to eat on the road. Mentally he calculated the time he would need to drive to the larger town, see how Henry was doing, reassure or comfort the family as appropriate and be back in time to deliver the eleven o'clock service. One leftover of his days in the corporate world was the way his mind instantly kicked into gear when a crisis arose.

He rounded the corner from the hallway to the kitchen and was surprised and relieved to see Megan there, kneading dough.

"Henry Epstein's in the hospital," he said, helping himself to coffee from the pot she'd obviously just brewed. "I'm heading over to Eagle River. Could you call the choir director and let her know I might be late for services?"

"What happened?" She set the dough in a pan to rise and pulled off her apron.

"Rick said something about a heart attack."

"Let me just leave a note for Reba and I'll go with you. We can call Fran Peters once we're on the road. She gets up with the rooster." She pulled on a heavy wool shirt that Reba kept by the back door and grabbed a banana and napkin. "Bring your coffee. I'll drive while you eat something and make the calls. Rick and his mom must be frantic with worry."

She was out the door and behind the wheel of her rusting car before he could protest. By the time he climbed into the passenger seat, she'd found her keys in the purse she apparently kept hidden under the front seat and started the engine. When she reached the end of the drive and turned left instead of right as he had expected, Jeb spoke up.

"He's in Eagle River, not Boulder Junction."

"Got it. I know a short cut. Call Fran and ask her to also call Reba in half an hour so she can put the bread in to bake. We had a couple of late guests come in last night."

"That's why you were up at this hour?"

Megan smiled. "I'm up by six most mornings. It's an old habit. I like the time before everyone starts to stir. I like the quiet—the mist rising off the lake, the birds going about their morning chores, the lack of human interruption. Of course, once the season starts in earnest I'm up because we need to get started baking and making sure things are ready for our guests."

Jeb nodded as he carefully balanced his mug of coffee against the twists and turns of the narrow back road she'd taken. "When I was in the corporate world, I used to get to work by six every morning. No one else was there at that hour and I found I did my best work then. What I could accomplish in that ninety minutes before the phone calls and e-mails and other employees started arriving was sometimes amazing."

"What company did you work for?"

"Ever hear of Mogul Pharmaceuticals?"

"Sure. They came out with that new cancer drug a few years back." She glanced at him. "You did that?"

"Not technically, but yeah, I was heading up the company when they launched that. I was also in charge when the drug had to be pulled off the market two years later," he admitted.

"I never understood that. I mean, if it worked then why…"

"Statistically speaking it didn't work often enough to make up for the risk of side effects."

"Still, if I had a terminal cancer diagnosis, I'd be willing to take that risk."

"That's what some patients thought until they experienced the side effects and, in some cases, died anyway. Then there were lawsuits and the shareholders got nervous, and the company had plenty of less risky products on the market and in the pipeline. So the board made a business decision and pulled it off the market."

"But it wasn't a business decision," Megan argued. "If the medicine saved one life…"

Jeb drained the last of the coffee, set the mug on the floor between his feet and peeled the banana. He broke off a piece and handed it to her. "That's not how it works."

She chewed her banana in silence, her expression one of deep concentration on either navigating the road or digesting his last comment. He waited for a debate on the pros and cons of business versus human need. He was actually enjoying their discussion.

"So, is that why you left corporate America for the ministry? Because you no longer believed in what you were doing?"

She had slowed the car to accommodate the posted speed limit as they entered the town of Eagle River.

"It's one reason," he admitted, but his reasons for entering the ministry were far too complex for the five minutes they might have now. "Is that the hospital up ahead there?"

"Yeah," she said, and seemed to have accepted his response at face value. "I'll drop you off and park, then meet you in the ICU. Just take a left to the elevators inside the front entrance. The ICU waiting room is on the third floor."

He was relieved to be back on the safe ground of coming to the aid of mutual friends. "Sounds like you've been here before."

"Once or twice," she muttered as she pulled up to the front entrance. She did not look at him, and Jeb realized that he wasn't the only one who was haunted by memories stirred either by their conversation or this unexpected trip to the hospital at dawn. He felt the urge to reach out to her.

"Go on," she said softly. "They need you."

As soon as Megan exited the elevator, she saw Henry's wife, Ginny, and knew the news wasn't good. She was seated on a vinyl sofa with Jeb next to her, his arm around her shoulders as he spoke softly to her. She was tearing a tissue to shreds and nodding slowly.

"Dad's in surgery," Rick said, coming to meet Megan.

Megan stood on tiptoe to give the giant of a man a hug and held on when she felt his shoulders sag and shudder. A set of automatic doors swung open with a burst of air at the far end of the corridor and Rick released her as he turned to face the surgeon coming their way. Ginny stood and Megan noticed that Jeb stood with her, his arm resting loosely around her shoulders. The doctor wore scrubs and did not look directly at them. Megan's heart plummeted at the same time she heard the air rush out of Rick's lungs as he crossed the room in two steps to tower over the doctor.

He spoke to Ginny and Rick at some length and she reached for her son's hand and held on. She nodded repeatedly and remained dry-eyed while tears rolled silently down Rick's cheeks unheeded. Megan saw that Jeb's long fingers had tightened on Ginny's shoulder and that he was asking the doctor questions. She waited for the surgeon to leave and then went to Ginny, who had collapsed onto a chair.

"She'll be all right," she told Jeb, and nodded toward the distraught Rick.

Like a time-lapse sequence in a film, gradually the

room filled. A social worker came and explained the next steps to Ginny. The funeral director was called. Ginny's sister and Henry's three siblings arrived with their families. And through it all Megan watched as Jeb quietly took charge, gently guiding Ginny, Rick and their family through the first steps of saying goodbye to a loved one.

Meanwhile she did what she did best. She fetched coffee. She sat with the family member who seemed to most need her. She slid a box of tissues from one side of the table to another, depending on the need. She placed her wool shirt-jacket around Ginny's thin shoulders when it seemed she could not stop shaking.

"Megan?"

She looked up and saw Jeb motioning to her from across the room. He pocketed his cell phone and stepped into the hallway, away from the others.

"I need you to do me a favor," he said.

"Of course."

"I tried calling Fran, but she's already left for the church and she won't hear the phone in the office."

Megan nodded. The choir director liked to arrive early and run through the hymn selections and her prelude before others arrived.

"Would you go back—go to the church and tell Fran what's happened. Ask her if she's okay with making today's service into a hymn sing and meditation. Jasper should be there by now. As an elder he can lead folks in a couple of readings."

She could practically hear the wheels turning as he put together the plan. She couldn't help thinking that he must have been a very effective business executive. Already this morning he had dealt with the necessary procedural details, all the time making sure that Ginny, Rick and other family members were comforted in their grief. Meanwhile he was remembering that he had an entire congregation expecting to show up for services in little more than an hour. "I'll leave right away."

"And, Megan?"

She had already pressed the elevator button as he pulled off his crewneck sweater and placed it over her shoulders. "My Bible is on the desk in my room with the passage for today's scripture marked."

"I'll get it and give it to Jasper," she promised, as the elevator doors slid open with a soft ding.

"Actually," Jeb said, holding the doors as she stepped in, "why don't you read it? Close the service with it and ask everyone to stand in silent prayer for a moment after."

Megan's eyes widened. "I couldn't…I…"

"I'm counting on you," he said with a smile, and let the doors slide shut.

As she hurried out to her car, Megan reprimanded herself for all the questions she should have asked. Should she tell Jasper to explain to the congregation why the new minister was missing the service? Should she come back for Jeb after the service? Should she…

Doubts assailed her, as they always did when someone assumed she'd have no problem delivering what they had requested. She steered with one hand while rummaging for her cell phone in the glove compartment, where she kept it to avoid the temptation to use it for anything other than an emergency. That had been the deal when Faith had urged her to buy a pay-as-you-go plan. "See, Mom? No contract. No worries."

"Emergencies only," Megan had insisted.

"But Mom, calls are free after nine most nights and on weekends," Faith had countered.

"The phone stays in the car."

Faith had rolled her eyes, then grinned and hugged Megan. "You worry way too much, you know."

Megan had only needed to arch one eyebrow before Faith had capitulated. "Fine. I'll make my calls from the car. That way we'll be sure to have it handy when that emergency comes up."

"Well, this is an emergency," Megan said, as she used her thumb to press the number for the inn. To her relief, Reba answered on the first ring.

"I heard," Reba said as soon as Megan started to deliver the news. "How's Ginny holding up?"

"She's a rock. Rick, on the other hand…"

"He was so close to his dad, poor thing."

Megan quickly explained Jeb's plan for services.

"You go on up to the church and tell the others. I'll get Jeb's Bible and send Faith up there with it."

"And a change of clothes," Megan added. "I'm still in my jeans."

"Got it. Now hang up and drive," Reba ordered, and the phone went dead.

One of Henry and Ginny's nephews dropped Jeb off at the church just as the congregation was singing what had to be the final hymn. Jeb had thought about stopping first at the inn to change, but he wanted to be there as the people were leaving the service. He wasn't sure how upset the townspeople were going to be. The news of Henry's sudden death had come as a real shock to many who had known him as a vibrant and charming man. He'd been a true pillar of the community.

He slipped into the back row, nodding to the Singer family, who slid closer together to make room for him. There was that moment of quiet commotion as everyone settled back into their pews, slid hymnals into the wooden holders and focused their attention once again on the pulpit at the front of the sanctuary as the final notes of Fran's transitional music faded.

The empty pulpit.

Jeb craned his neck, looking for Megan, and spotted her cap of honey-brown hair. She was seated alone on the front pew. Slowly she rose and, moving as if her legs were made of wood, she stepped up two shallow stairs onto the platform. She was carrying his Bible, one index finger marking the page.

She reached the podium and took her time opening the Bible and setting it on the stand. She was seemingly unaware of the few hushed whispers that followed her.

"Please rise for the benediction," she said, her voice small but audible.

As one the congregation came to its feet. Every head bowed and the only sound was the wind rustling the willow tree outside the east windows.

"To everything there is a season," Megan began hesitantly, "and a time to every purpose under Heaven."

Jeb closed his eyes as the familiar words from the third chapter of Paul's letter to the Ephesians rolled across the church like a wave on a beach. With every repetition of the phrasing "a time," Megan's voice gained confidence and strength. He had chosen this passage because his intent had been to tie the familiar scripture to the changing of the seasons—the coming of spring, the promise of summer, the distant call of autumn that would carry the village back to the quiet serenity of winter. How could he have imagined that it would be the eulogy for a man who had been his friend only a few weeks, but had left his mark all the same?

He thought of how a professor in seminary had warned his students that dealing with death would be among their greatest challenges. At the time Jeb had thought that he had an advantage over most of the other students. He had experienced death in all its cold and dark mystery firsthand. Only now did he truly understand what the professor had been saying. For although he had been the one in need of comfort and explanations before, now he would be the one people would expect to make sense of what God could possibly have been thinking to take such a good and decent man from them in his prime.

He opened his eyes as Megan uttered the final verse. She looked directly at him, then bowed her head as Jasper slipped into the vestibule and yanked hard on the thick rope attached to the church bell. Twelve times it tolled as a community stood shoulder to shoulder to pay silent tribute to their friend and neighbor, Henry Epstein.

Chapter Five

"Lovely service, Reverend Matthews," Megan heard Nellie Barnsworth tell Jeb. Nellie had the kind of voice that carried beyond surrounding noise. Neither the chatter of other church members nor the final notes of Fran's postlude could cover the older woman's next pronouncement. "I do wonder that you didn't ask Jessica Burbank to read that last passage though. Don't get me wrong. Megan has a lovely soft voice and, of course, being new here you may not have known."

"Known what, Mrs. Barnsworth?"

"Why, Jessica is such a gifted actress. We couldn't do without her in our little community players group. Next time," she added as she started down the front stairs, calling out to her husband to lend her a hand.

Megan saw Jeb turn his attention to the next couple exiting the church, accepting the man's handshake and inclining his head sympathetically as the woman asked how Ginny Epstein was holding up.

There were three people between her and the front door—between her and Jeb. Megan thought of the way

Jeb had been looking at her when she'd glanced up from the reading. She'd been surprised to see him there in the last pew, as if he were simply another member of the congregation. But the way he'd watched her, his expression had been unreadable. Was that because he hadn't expected her to read the passage well? Had he had second thoughts about entrusting her with a key portion of the spontaneous service? Megan retraced her steps and slipped out the side door.

She paused for a moment at the railing of the ramp that made the historic church accessible to members like Reba who had trouble managing the steep front steps. She was trying to decide her next move. To return to the inn she would have to walk past the front entrance. Jeb would see her. He might even call her over so he could thank her for taking a role in the service, as she'd heard him thank Jasper. She was considering heading for the basement community room to help close up after Sunday School classes when she heard Faith's laughter.

Megan followed the sound and turned the corner of the church to find Faith and Caleb Armstrong, oblivious to anyone but each other, their foreheads nearly touching. His hands were braced flat against the church wall to either side of her daughter's narrow shoulders. Faith's breath was coming in quick little gasps of excitement, judging from the steady rise and fall of her chest.

"Why, Caleb," Megan called out in an overly cheerful tone, which startled the young people to attention. "I didn't realize your family had opened the summer house for the season."

"Hello, Ms. Osbourne." Caleb took a step back from Faith, who was now glowering at her mother. "I just came up for the weekend with some friends. We're supposed to be studying for exams, so…" He shrugged and gave Megan a charming smile that she was sure worked magic on most women.

But Megan didn't like Caleb Armstrong. Not that he'd given her cause. He was always polite, and his grandparents had begun summering in the area before Megan was born. Still, there was something about his interaction with Faith that rattled every protective bone in Megan's body. He'd first taken notice of Faith the previous fall, and Faith had been thrilled by his attention. She liked to point out that she was a year younger than he was. But Megan was well aware that age, when one party was a high school junior and the other a graduating senior, could be far too large a gap.

"The whole Armstrong clan will come up to stay later in June," he added when Megan made no comment. He glanced at Faith. "So, be seeing you around?"

"Sure," Faith said. "You know where to find me," she added with a coquettish smile that made Megan bristle.

Caleb chuckled and started toward a baby-blue convertible parked at an angle so that it occupied three spaces. "Nice seeing you again, Ms. O," he called with a wave.

"Okay, that was embarrassing," Faith mumbled. But she continued to smile and wave as if the boy were leaving for war instead of his parents' log house on the far side of the lake.

"I have nothing against Caleb Armstrong," Megan said, mentally asking forgiveness for the lie.

Faith rolled her eyes. "Really? Coulda fooled me."

"Watch your tone, missy," Megan snapped, sounding more like Reba than herself.

"Sorry," both said at the same time.

"I thought you trusted me," Faith added.

"I do, honey," Megan assured her. *It's him I don't trust.*

"Mom, I'm not stupid. I know Caleb's interest is more physical than anything else. He's a guy, right?" She grinned, and in that grin Megan saw the little girl she'd raised to be strong and smart and self-assured.

"So what's the appeal?"

Faith shrugged. "I like him. He's smart and funny and different from the boys around here. Hey, maybe it's more of a challenge. I want him to see beyond the blooming bod. I want him to see that a girl from Singing Springs is not just some hick. I may not be as worldly as his other friends, but I'm way more interesting."

Megan hugged Faith hard. "How did I get so lucky to have a daughter like you?" she whispered.

"Ah, Mom." Faith pulled away and laughed. "You worry way too much." She hooked the hobo cloth bag that Reba had made her over one shoulder. "I have to go," she said. "I promised Aunt Reba I'd handle the phone and front desk while she goes over to see Mrs. Epstein."

"Okay. I'll see you later."

Megan watched Faith race off down the hill, her skirt flying around her long legs and her golden ponytail swinging from side to side.

"There you are." Jeb's footsteps had been silenced by the bark mulch that lined the path around the church. "I've been looking for you everywhere."

"Here I am," Megan repeated.

"I wanted to tell you how very special I thought your reading of the scripture was this morning. It was…"

"I just read the words," Megan protested. "I'm just glad you selected a passage that I was familiar with."

A slight frown furrowed Jeb's brow and he took a

moment before he said anything more. "You touched people's hearts, Megan," he said quietly. "You made familiar scripture fresh for them. That's a gift."

Megan felt the heat rush to her cheeks. "How's Ginny?" she asked, casting about for anything that would take his attention off her.

"She's an amazing woman," Jeb replied. "For now she seems to be leaning on Rick. I think she understands that he needs that now."

Megan nodded. "Rick and his father were very close." She thought of how envious she had sometimes been of that closeness. "It's not going to be easy for him. I mean, Henry's death was so sudden and unexpected."

Jeb looked away, but not before Megan saw the expression of abject sadness cross his face that she had noticed before. She placed her hand on his arm. "Rick respects you, Jeb, and he's going to need help making sense of this."

"I'm on my way over there now. Do you want to come along? Maybe while I have a few minutes with Rick, you could be there for Ginny?"

It occurred to Megan that perhaps in the city, where Jeb had lived a good portion of his adult life, things might be different. But here in Singing Springs, she was well aware that the Epstein house was probably already crowded with neighbors and friends and extended family. "Ginny's not alone," she assured him. "Reba's there and probably half the congregation by now."

She saw by his surprised but pleased look that she had read the situation accurately. "It's a small town, Jeb. We're all like family here."

He smiled and shook his head. "That'll take some getting used to, but it does sound nice."

Megan laughed. "Be careful what you wish for, Reverend. That small-town closeness can also sometimes get to be a little cloying. You'll soon get the hang of who's who and what role each person has been assigned," she teased.

"Like Jessica Burbank is the actress?" He was watching her closely, his expression serious once again. "I saw you waiting in line. You heard Mrs. Barnsworth's comments?"

"Everyone within shouting distance hears Nellie when she decides she needs to make a point," Megan assured him. "And the truth is that Jessica is truly talented. If you thought I did a passable job, you would have been blown away by Jessica."

"I never said 'passable,' Megan."

"The point is that in small towns people have their roles to play—no pun intended."

"You mean they get labeled."

"That's another way to look at it—a negative way though. Look, folks mean well and you just have to keep that in mind."

"Sounds like you've had some practice." He braced one hand against the wall of the church as if settling in for a long discussion.

Megan met his gaze. "I live here, Jeb. I've lived my whole life here, and I expect I'm as prone as anyone to label and cast people in the roles that best suit them. There's no harm meant—or taken."

To her surprise, Jeb grinned. "You know what, Ms. Osbourne? If I had met you back when I was in the business world, I would have hired you on the spot."

"As what?"

He narrowed his eyes as if sizing her up for a job. "Something to do with understanding people, for sure.

Maybe something in human resources. No, market research."

Megan laughed. "I'm not sure what market research is, but I think I'll pass, thank you. Now, if that ride to Ginny's is still available, I'll take you up on it."

Jeb pushed himself away from the building and gave her a slight bow. "Your chariot awaits, ma'am."

The next two weeks were jam-packed with preparing his sermons and the eulogy for Henry's funeral, plus helping Rick complete repairs to the parsonage. Jeb was relieved to see that working on the roof seemed therapeutic for Rick, rather than a challenge to his grief, as Jeb had feared. Jeb was well acquainted with the toll grief could take. It had been his constant companion ever since the deaths of his wife and child. But on the morning he was scheduled to move back to the parsonage, Jeb realized that he had gone for days without once feeling the familiar stabbing pain of loss.

However, he was well aware that he could not bury his memories and regrets on this day. This was Memorial Day, the anniversary of the accident that had changed Jeb's life forever. As usual, he planned the hours very carefully, staging them to simply get him to tomorrow.

The move would take only an hour. Over the two weeks he'd been staying at the inn he'd brought down several boxes of books and papers as well as more of his clothes, but everything would fit in his car for the trip back to the parsonage. Everyone in town was excited about the annual parade and picnic in the park to kick off the tourist season. He doubted if anyone would miss him. His plan was to pack up his things, then go to the lakeside trail where he'd walked with Megan and spend a quiet morning in meditation and prayer.

But apparently God had other ideas about how the day might go, as Jeb discovered as soon as he went into the kitchen for breakfast.

"Oh, Jeb, you're just the person we need," Reba exclaimed, as she dished up blueberry pancakes and set a plate and pitcher of syrup in front of him. "Ty and Minnie Glover were scheduled to lead the parade with their horse-drawn buggy, but now Nellie—the horse, not the woman—has pulled up lame. Jasper has offered one of his antique cars as a substitute, but since he's the parade marshal, Nellie—his wife, not the horse—insists that it's only proper for the two of them to be driven through town in Jasper's vintage Thunderbird." She poured coffee for him without a break in her explanation. "I told Jasper that I'd see to it. Poor henpecked man, I thought he was going to burst into tears of gratitude."

She set the coffeepot back on its heating unit and plopped a man's black derby hat on Jeb's head. "Perfect. I told Megan you would be perfect for the part. She, of course, was bound and determined to drive the car herself, but I told her she could not go against history, and at the turn of the century no woman was driving in this community. Not that I recall personally, you understand," she huffed. "I'm assuming you can handle a stick shift on a Model T Ford?"

Jeb took a swallow of his coffee just in case any response he made was interrupted by more of Reba's monologue. When she remained silent, impatiently tapping one foot, he cleared his throat. "I've driven stick, but have to admit I've never driven a Model T before."

Reba dismissed that with a wave of her hand. "A car is a car. Faith!" she shouted.

There was a stirring in the laundry room and the teenager stuck her head around the corner. "I'm right here," she said.

"Good. As soon as you finish ironing that shirt take it to Jeb's room." She turned back to Jeb. "Your black suit pants will work. It would be best if you had a handlebar mustache, but no matter. Suspenders," she muttered and limped down the hall.

"Faith?" Jeb called out.

"Coming," the girl replied and came around the corner with a crisp white collarless shirt on a hanger.

"Want to tell me what's going on?"

"On the surface or behind the scenes?"

"Both."

The girl hooked the shirt hanger over the top of the door and perched on a high stool. "Okay, on the surface she's saving the day, making sure the parade is not a disappointment for anyone. She's thinking that you, Mom and I will get all dressed up like it was 1910 or something and lead the parade through town, driving Mr. Barnsworth's Model T that will be all decked out in bunting and flags and such."

"And underneath?"

"Uncle Stan—Reba's late husband—was the founder of the parade. It was like his baby, the way he made sure every detail was taken care of. He believed it was the kickoff to the season and that if he made it special enough it would draw people here from all over. They would talk about what a good time they had and come back. And since he died…"

"Reba has taken it on," Jeb guessed.

"Pretty much," Faith said, sliding off the stool. "Will you do it? It would mean a lot to Reba."

"Of course," Jeb said, as he carried his dishes to the sink, rinsed them and loaded them into the dishwasher. Through the window he saw Megan coming toward the inn. She was wearing a long skirt covered by a tan duster coat, and she was clinging to an oversize lady's hat festooned with yards of netting.

"Faith, you need to get dressed," she said as soon as she was inside the back door. "We have to leave now if we're going to…"

Faith held up the freshly ironed shirt and nodded toward Jeb. "Auntie Reba has hired us a chauffeur."

Just then Reba came rushing back, waving a pair of red suspenders. "Stan used these when he was a volunteer fireman. They'll have to do," she said. "Oh, Megan, don't you look lovely. Isn't she just a picture, Jeb?"

In the weeks since he had moved into the inn, Reba had not let up on her campaign to throw Megan and Jeb together at every turn. He saw Megan's mouth tighten with exasperation. "I think I need to see the whole picture," he said, relieving her of the hat and placing it on her head, then tying the long streamers into a large floppy bow.

He'd meant to lighten the moment, to show her that he was well aware of Reba's intent and found it simply amusing. But he suddenly realized that he had never stood quite this close to her. Close enough to be aware of the flecks of gold that gave her eyes that sparkle he'd always thought the result of her dimples. Close enough to be charmed by the faint sprinkling of freckles across her cheeks. Close enough to be enveloped by the scent of lavender that brought to mind spring showers and gentle warm winds.

He finished tying the bow and took a step back. "A picture," he agreed, "right out of the history books."

Outside, an engine backfired and chugged as it labored up the drive.

"That'll be Jasper. Now, Faith, honey, get yourself changed," Reba instructed as she hustled the girl from the room. "You, too, Reverend," she called.

"You don't have to do this," Megan said. "I can drive the car and…"

"Ah, but according to Reba that would be historically incorrect," Jeb said as he unhooked the shirt hanger, picked up the suspenders and headed back down the hall to his room. "Besides, it sounds like fun," he called, just before he closed the door.

"Fun?" Megan muttered, staring after him. Did the man not get it? Did it not occur to him that Reba's plan was to have the three of them drive through town as if they were a family? Husband, wife and daughter? Did it not occur to him that there would be those in town who would hardly think Megan was the kind of woman he ought to be seen with?

The trouble was that she liked Jeb—more than liked him. She was attracted to him in a way she had not felt in years. But she recognized the impossibility of such a match, even if he found her attractive, as well. Which she was pretty sure he did, but in a friendly way. The very idea that a man like him would even consider someone like her was preposterous.

She bustled about, putting the kitchen and laundry room in order and praying. "I know this day is special for Reba, dear God, but I really need Your help here. In the past her matchmaking has been limited to hints and thinly veiled glances and such. This is a step up and, well, it's embarrassing. And furthermore, there's my own weakness when it comes to the man. Part of the problem here is that I can't help wishing…"

"How do I look?"

Megan jumped as Jeb pushed back the door of the laundry room and struck a pose, the derby cocked at a jaunty angle and his thumbs looped beneath the bright red suspenders. But it was the bold black mark on his upper lip that made Megan burst into laughter.

"What is that?" she crowed.

Jeb looked wounded, but then he grinned. "Reba wanted a mustache."

"But it's black and your hair isn't," she pointed out.

"Thus the derby," he replied, pulling the hat more firmly in place to cover his hair.

Megan took a step closer and stood on tiptoe to more closely examine the mustache. "Is that—tell me you didn't use a marker," she said as she ran her finger over his upper lip.

Just then Faith came hurrying into the kitchen, and Megan practically leaped away from Jeb as if they had been caught in a compromising moment. "I…wait till you see…" she stuttered, taking Jeb's arm to turn him so Faith could get the full effect.

But Faith was scowling at the two of them and barely paused on her way out the back door. "Mr. Barnsworth is here," she said. "In case you didn't notice, Mother."

"Faith," Megan called, starting after her. Her daughter only called her Mother when she was upset. It was not a term of endearment.

"She misread the moment," Jeb assured her. "When she sees this—" he pointed to his lip "—she'll understand."

But Jeb's words did nothing to reassure Megan. As a little girl Faith had made it clear she was opposed to anything upsetting the balance of an all-female household. Gone was the grandfather whose moods and love Faith could never be sure of. Gone was the father she'd never known. In Faith's world, security came in the female form.

In those early years, whenever Megan had begun seeing a man, Faith had made her displeasure known. Over time it just became easier not to date—not just because it upset Faith, but frankly because it was just too hard. Megan didn't trust male/female relationships any more than her daughter did. She'd always thought that once Faith was older there would be time to explore the possibility of romance.

But unlike the child who had clung to her and begged her not to go when a man had come calling, this girl marched straight through the kitchen and out the back door with a kind of self-righteous confidence that scared Megan. After all, hadn't that been the promise she'd made God after Danny had abandoned them? *Help me raise this child—this precious gift—to be strong and kind and confident, and I'll never ask another thing for myself.*

Chapter Six

"Faith!"

The girl had climbed into the rumble seat of the antique car and folded her arms tightly across her chest. On an ordinary day Megan might have taken this as a reaction to the chilly May morning, but the scowl on her daughter's beautiful face told her it wasn't the weather. Jeb and Jasper were standing in front of the car, deep in conversation about the mechanics of driving a Model T.

"Faith, I don't know what you thought you saw back in the kitchen just now, but…"

"Hey, I get it. It's fine for you to cozy up to the new minister, but if I so much as speak to Caleb it's like a federal case or something."

"That's unfair and unlike you."

"If Caleb and I share a private moment that's cause for calling out the National Guard. But if you and Reverend McDreamboat over there…" She jerked her head in Jeb's direction.

"That's enough, young lady." One of Megan's main

concerns about Faith spending so much time with Caleb and his friends was the difference she saw in her daughter's demeanor afterward. There was a new hint of cynicism and sarcasm.

Megan saw Jeb glance their way, his eyebrows lifted in a question. Megan turned her attention back to Faith. "This isn't the time to discuss this, but understand one thing. Reverend Matthews is our friend and our pastor—nothing more." She saw a flicker of wanting to believe in Faith's eyes. "And for the record I have nothing against you and Caleb being friends. I just worry—as any mother would—that he's older."

"Gee, two whole years," Faith muttered.

"There are times when two whole years might as well be ten," Megan said as she reached back and took her daughter's hand. "Hey, I just don't want you to get hurt, okay?"

"I'm not a kid."

"No, you're not, and that's part of the problem."

"Are we all set back there?" Jeb called.

Faith looked up for the first time since storming out to the car. "What is that thing on his lip?" she whispered, trying hard not to laugh.

"Reba wanted a mustache," Megan explained.

As Jeb moved closer Faith leaned forward. "That's like a permanent marker," she announced. "You are so never going to get that off."

"Sure I will," Jeb said with a grin. He reached up and stripped off his upper lip the length of invisible tape he'd drawn the mustache on and cut to exact shape. "Nothing to it," he said as he pressed the fake mustache back in place and climbed into the car. "All set," he called as Jasper cranked up the engine.

* * *

Everyone declared the parade to be the best ever and Jeb was glad that he'd agreed to help out. The truth was that he'd been glad for the diversion. In the years since Deborah and Sally died, he'd always spent the day dwelling on his loss, blaming himself for the many times he had chosen work over his family, and praying for God's guidance in atoning for those past mistakes.

He looked out over the crowd gathered at the lake park. They were enjoying the free cups of ice cream the Shack had donated and catching up with some of the regular summer residents who used the holiday weekend to open their cottages and cabins for the summer. He couldn't help but reflect on how much his life had changed. He wasn't all the way there yet, but he was on the right path. And then he saw Megan Osbourne.

She was sitting on top of a picnic table, her feet resting on the wooden seat as she fed ice cream to a small child sitting next to her. She was still wearing the duster, although she'd abandoned the hat. Even at a distance Jeb picked out the sound of her laughter from all the other chatter that surrounded him.

He recognized the two women with Megan. One was a waitress at the local diner and the other was a young mother whose husband had helped Rick finish the roofing repairs. One was a woman Megan had known all her life and the other was new to the community.

Watching the exchange, Jeb realized that Megan had two distinct personalities when she was around others. Sometimes, like now, she was totally at ease, laughing, leaning into the conversation while she multitasked, feeding the child and taking an occasional bite of ice cream for herself. But Jeb had also noticed that there were times when Megan was more withdrawn. It wasn't so much shyness as insecurity. And yet the woman Jeb had come to know as he'd worked with her planting flower beds or handling minor repairs around the inn was spirited and funny and smart. More than once she had startled him with her insights regarding some church member or neighbor that he was struggling to understand.

"You can't take Myrtle Taft at face value," she had coached him one afternoon as they replaced storm windows with screens. "She's taught seventh grade here for forty-some years. Being a teacher in a small town means she's as likely to run into her students at the grocery as she is to see them in class. Myrtle believes that it's important not to be one person in the classroom and another out in public, so she long ago chose to be the schoolmarm no matter the circumstances."

Jeb had thought about that and had begun treating Mrs. Taft with an extra dose of respect and deference. And to his surprise the woman had warmed to him immediately. In fact, just the day before she'd stopped at the church and handed him an envelope.

"Megan Osbourne mentioned that you were thinking of setting up some sort of social gathering place for the teens. Believe me, pastor, with the influx of summer folks influencing our local youth, those youngsters will bear watching. You'll need to buy some equipment, I expect—a television with one of those video game players. I priced them out and this should cover the cost of a nice one. All I ask is that you supervise the selection of games. Some of them can be quite violent, you know."

Jeb had listened to this lecture politely and thanked her

for her generous donation, although he had not opened the sealed envelope until much later that evening. The amount of the check had been staggering. One thousand dollars. He'd been tempted to call Megan and share the news with her, but it had been after eleven and…

"Well, you can tell her now," he said as he saw Megan hand the child back to his mother. Then Megan headed toward the booth where Reba was handing out small American flags to passersby.

"Megan!"

She paused and looked back at him. She had a way of looking up at people as if she were wearing a hood and needed to take care not to reveal too much of her expression. She was doing that now, but then he saw a smile twitch at the corners of her mouth. Whatever had been going on with Faith earlier seemed to have passed. Megan was relaxed and clearly enjoying the day.

Jeb grinned as he fell into step with her. "I wanted to tell you…" he began.

"Reba needs…" she said at the same moment and then she laughed. "You first."

"I thought we should start making some plans for the youth center," he said, taking her elbow to steer her past a group of young people sprawled across the grass and oblivious to anyone but themselves. "Myrtle Taft has kicked us off with a sizeable donation."

"Really?"

"A thousand dollars," he added, and waited for her to express the same shock and awe he had felt upon seeing the check.

"That's nice," was her only response. Her attention had been drawn to a far corner of the park where Faith and a tall, strapping boy were walking toward the lake, their arms wrapped tightly around each other's waists. "Would you excuse me?"

She would have started after them, but for reasons he didn't fully understand, Jeb reached out and took her hand, stopping her. "She'll be fine," he said. "She's your daughter."

Rather than reassure her, his words seemed to cause Megan more doubt. "Caleb Armstrong is older and more sophisticated," she explained. "She likes him and she's flattered by his attention. That can be dangerous for someone her age—even a girl as bright and confident as Faith."

"Tell you what, you go check in with Reba and let me handle this, okay?"

The surprise he'd expected when he told her about Myrtle's check had been nothing compared to the look of sheer astonishment she gave him now. "I really don't see…"

"We need help organizing a youth center, right? Who better to give us a hand in appealing to the summer teens than Mr. Leader of the Pack there?"

"I… He… It'll never work."

"Ooh, you just laid down a challenge I can't resist, lady. Watch this." Jeb took several long strides toward the two young people. "Hey!" he shouted. "Are you Caleb Armstrong?" he added when Faith and Caleb glanced back.

Jeb saw Faith say something to Caleb, and then the boy smiled broadly and started back up the hill toward Jeb. "Yes, sir, I am," he said extending a handshake.

"Just the man I've been hoping to meet," Jeb said as he shook the boy's hand. "I'm the minister of the Chapel on the Hill—Jeb Matthews. Faith's mom suggested that if anyone could give me advice for a project we want to get started at the church, it would be you. Do you and Faith have some time now?"

"Sure," Caleb replied without so much as a glance at Faith. "How can I help?"

Jeb had read the young man exactly right. In his years in the corporate world he'd met a lot of guys like Caleb—eager to make their mark, good at sizing up opportunities that might help them impress those who held some power, oblivious to those whose affections they'd already won. Jeb knew how someone like Caleb Armstrong operated because he had once been exactly that kind of person.

Megan saw Faith cast her a belligerent look. She took the easy way out, shrugging her shoulders as she looked back at Jeb and Caleb and then headed over to Reba's booth.

"Oh, Megan, bless you. Could you take over for a few minutes and let me catch my breath?" Reba said as she plopped down on a stool and inhaled deeply several times. "I think this is the biggest crowd we've ever had for the parade," she added, beaming up at Megan. "Stan would be so pleased."

Megan put her arm around the older woman's shoulders. "I'm sure he's looking down on us all right now. Who do you think asked God to send us such a beautiful day?" She gave Reba a quick hug then turned to distribute flags to a crowd of tourists.

"So what's with Jeb and the Armstrong boy?" Reba asked when there was a break in the line for a free flag.

Megan shook her head. "I think he's trying to get him involved in the youth center project."

"Good idea."

Megan lifted one eyebrow.

"Ah, you don't think so?"

"I don't know. Maybe. It's just that it seems like another possibility for throwing Faith and Caleb together."

"It also is something that might pique Faith's interest in getting more involved at church—something, I would remind you, that you've worried about in the past."

Megan grinned. "You always were a glass-half-full kind of person."

Reba took Megan's hand. "Honey, here's what I know. You have done a good job raising that child and there comes a time when you have to give her the wings to try flying through life on her own. And there's a bonus in that for you, as well."

"And that is?"

Reba winked. "You finally have time to give a little thought to what the rest of your life might look like once your fledgling is out on her own."

"Oh, Reba, thanks to you I have a wonderful life—everything I could possibly want is right here in Singing Springs."

"Nothing stays the same, honey," Reba said. "Change is a fact of life, and it could be that God's tagged you for something you've been preparing for your whole life without even realizing it." She pushed herself to her feet and took Megan's cluster of flags from her. "Okay, break's over and that's about my quota of sage advice for the day. Why don't you go enjoy the festivities? Oh, look, here comes Jeb. Like I always say, timing is everything."

Megan glanced up and indeed Jeb was heading straight for the flag booth, his smile as bright as the sun itself.

"We have a committee," he said, his tone as triumphant as his smile.

"Caleb Armstrong?"

"Caleb and Faith plus you and me. It's a start."

"It sure sounds that way," Reba agreed. "Now, why don't the two of you take this discussion over there by the lemonade stand so I can get back to handing out these flags. Shoo." She gave Megan a gentle shove in Jeb's direction and turned her attention to a passing group of young people.

"We probably need a couple more adults and maybe one more young person on the team," Jeb said. "How would you feel about asking Jessica Burbank and her daughter Cindy to be part of this?"

"Sure." *What was she going to say? No? It would be difficult for me?*

"Don't just give in, Megan." Jeb's tone had changed entirely. His voice was quiet but gentle. A counselor. A pastor.

"I'm not," she protested. "Jessica will be a wonderful addition. The kids in town all love her and she has such creative ideas."

"As do you," he said. "Jessica has a lot of respect for you, Megan. In fact, when I mentioned the idea of starting a youth center while we were at Henry's wake and told her I was hoping to have you chair the committee, she said I couldn't have made a better choice."

"So, you've already asked her to be part of this?"

"Nope. Just kicking around ideas. She did suggest Cindy as a person who might be a good bridge between the teens and 'tweens in town." He picked up two cups of lemonade from the table and handed one to her. "But it's your committee if you accept the chair position. You should really choose your own team."

"Oh, Jeb, I've never chaired anything in my life. There are so many others—Jessica for starters."

"So, you're saying no?"

His disappointment was so obvious that Megan had trouble meeting his eyes. "I'm saying you can do better," she murmured.

"I don't agree, but it's your call." He took a drink of his lemonade, but when she glanced up his eyes were focused on her, challenging her, daring her.

"Oh, all right, but…"

He grinned. "Nope. No codicils. You've agreed, now let's get to work." He pulled out the BlackBerry he'd once told them was a holdover from his days in the corporate world and studied it. "How's tomorrow night for a first meeting?"

"It's a school night and, besides, Caleb is supposed to head back to Milwaukee tonight. He won't be back until after graduation, when his family comes up in June."

"Well, we can't wait until June to get this thing going."

"We could meet later today—maybe have a light supper before Caleb heads back?" Megan couldn't help thinking this would allow Faith and Caleb to be together but remove the temptation to give in to teenage angst over the time that would pass before they'd see each other again.

"Great idea. See? I knew you were a natural at this leadership thing."

Megan felt the warmth of his praise spread through her like syrup on waffles. "Maybe we could meet at the inn and include Jessica and Cindy," she added, taking further pleasure in the look of surprise that passed over his handsome features. "I mean, if you still think asking them to be part of the committee is a good idea."

"Sounds like a plan," he said and drained the last of his lemonade. "Six o'clock?"

"Sounds like a plan," Megan parroted his response. "I'll go tell Faith…and Caleb."

"Why don't you go invite Jessica and Cindy to the meeting?" he suggested. "I'll check in with Faith and Caleb. And then, if you're not busy, I thought maybe we could finish that walk along the nature trail we started several weeks ago."

Megan knew the difference between a minister counseling her, a cohort setting up a committee meeting and a man asking to spend time with her. Jeb was suggesting the latter. She became too aware of their surroundings. They were in the midst of locals who would surely take notice of all the time they'd already spent together today. And there was Faith, who had made no secret of her disagreement with Reba's attempts at matchmaking, not to mention Reba herself, who would no doubt take false hope in seeing Megan and Jeb go off together. She should refuse—nip in the bud any idea he might have of romantic involvement.

"Okay," she said, barely realizing she'd spoken aloud until she looked up and saw Jeb's smile.

"Okay," he repeated. And reflected in his gaze was the flicker of joy she felt at the idea that this man wanted to spend time with her—just to be with her.

"I don't know why you're so worried about Faith," she muttered to herself, as she headed toward where Jessica Burbank stood on the sidelines, watching her twins play soccer. "You're the one acting like a starry-eyed teenager."

* * *

Megan and Jessica greeted each other as they had for years. Their smiles were too wide, their voices too enthusiastic, their greeting generic.

"Perfect weather for the parade," Megan said as she stood next to Jessica on the sidelines.

"We couldn't have asked for better," Jessica agreed.

It was moments like these when memories of the friendship they had shared threatened to overwhelm Megan. She and Jessica had been the best of friends. As the school year wound to a close they had spent hours in Jessica's pink bedroom, planning their summer. The hours spent in those fairyland surroundings had been like an escape for Megan and had allowed her to forget the dark and dreary house she shared with her father.

"Goal!" Jessica shouted, pumping a fist high in the air and grinning at one of the twins.

Megan shook off her reverie and applauded the boy's achievement. As the teams lined up for a fresh start, Jessica sat on the blanket she'd spread on the sidelines and patted a place beside her. "Can you sit for a while?" She squinted up at Megan, the sun in her eyes, her long brown bangs further obstructing her vision.

"Remember that time we decided to cut each other's hair?" Megan said, accepting the invitation to sit.

Jessica looked surprised and then curious. "What made you think of that?"

Megan shrugged, embarrassed. What a dork, Faith would say. "I'm not sure—time of year, seeing the kids, memories."

"Yeah." Jessica pulled at a blade of grass on the edge of the blanket and gazed out at the soccer players. "It all goes so fast, doesn't it?"

They watched the action on the field for a long moment and then Megan found her courage. "I was wondering—that is, Reverend Matthews suggested—well, you may have heard that he wants to establish a youth center in the church basement. A place for the kids to gather and stay out of trouble."

"He mentioned something about that. Pete and I both think it's a great idea. How can we help?"

It was so like Jessica to cut to the chase. Megan couldn't help but smile. "Would you be willing to serve on the planning committee?"

"Sure." No questions to check who else might be on the committee.

"And Jeb—Reverend Matthews—thinks the young people should also be represented. He's already recruited Faith and Caleb Armstrong, so do you think Cindy might be—"

"Sure. Well, I'll check, but I'd say the chance to work on anything with Faith is its own reward. Cindy idolizes Faith."

Megan searched Jessica's tone and expression for any sign that this was a problem for her and found nothing but approval. But then a tiny frown creased Jessica's forehead. "Caleb Armstrong, you say?"

Megan nodded. "I think Jeb wants someone to represent the summer kids and Caleb seems to be their leader."

Jessica released a long sigh. "Yeah, it makes sense." She made a face and glanced at Megan. "Do you trust that kid?"

"Not really," Megan admitted.

"Well, good, because I worry about the attention he's been showering on Faith. He reminds me of Danny at that age."

Megan could not have been more shocked if Jessica had suddenly announced her intention to run away to Las Vegas and become a showgirl—something the two of them used to consider when they were teens and life in Singing Springs seemed beyond boring.

"I'm so sorry, Megan," Jessica said, covering Megan's hand with hers. "That was uncalled for."

"No, it's true. I mean, Caleb is handsome and smart and impossibly charming, as was Danny."

Jessica went back to pulling stray blades of grass. "I've missed you, Megan," she said softly.

And like the friends they had once been Megan didn't have to ask what she meant. "Me, too," she replied. "I'm really looking forward to working on the youth center with you. You wouldn't be interested in chairing the committee, would you?"

Jessica let out a honk of a laugh that had been her signature in high school, and Megan couldn't help grinning.

"Not on your life, Meggie. The hunk minister tapped you for this assignment so go forth and lead." Then she was on her feet again, shouting at one of the fathers refereeing the game, "Hey, Chad, ever hear of offsides?"

Megan saw Jessica's husband, Pete, signal her to hold back, but that simply wasn't Jessica. She saw someone in need of her help and she gave it—whether they asked for it or not. Megan smiled and wondered at the lightness she felt as she stood up. It felt as if she'd carried a huge rock around so long that she hadn't even realized she was hauling it. And then someone— Jessica—had come along and set it down for her. "Hey, Jess, we're meeting at the inn tonight at six, okay?"

Jessica acknowledged the information with a wave and kept on stalking the referee.

Megan lifted the long skirt of her costume and climbed the grassy hillside that surrounded the soccer field. When she reached the top Jeb was waiting.

"How did it go?"

"Fine. She and Cindy are on board."

"So, ready to take that walk?" He held his hand out to her, saw her hesitation and withdrew it. "It's a walk, Megan, okay?"

But Megan couldn't help noticing that Jeb seemed a little irritated, and that very human response to her slight made her realize that even a preacher could be vulnerable.

Chapter Seven

"How did things go with Jessica?" Jeb asked, forcing himself to focus on topics that might obscure his loss of patience earlier.

"It was as if we'd never stopped being friends," Megan marveled.

"Perhaps because you hadn't?"

She considered that for a long moment. "You're right. There wasn't any real break. Jess was already off at college. Of course, when she came home after her freshman year it was like we took up right where we'd left off—talking for hours and hanging out at her house the way we always had."

"And you and her brother were dating?"

"Danny was leaving for college that fall, and then I'd planned to go the year after that. Danny had a full athletic scholarship, and the guidance counselor had hinted I could qualify for an academic scholarship at the same school. The three of us used to dream about all being on campus together." She walked ahead of him on the narrow path, her hands clasped behind her back, her head bent with the weight of her memories. "It never happened. Danny got accepted to the University of Southern California and that was it," she murmured, then looked back at him with a smile. "Enough. The important thing is that Jess is going to help us get the youth center going. She's a wonder at organizing things."

They spent some time talking about the logistics of setting up a center in the cramped space of the church basement, and soon found themselves at the end of the circular trail. The festivities at the park were breaking up. Megan spotted Reba lifting a box loaded with leftover programs and flags into her van and ran off to help her. "See you at six," she called.

Jeb couldn't believe how quickly the day—the anniversary—had slipped by. Had he started to forget, to allow the memory of his wife and daughter to fade? And was that the natural way of things, or had he selfishly enjoyed the day in spite of its meaning?

At the meeting it was apparent how close the friendship between Megan and Jessica had once been. They were each brimming with ideas, talking over each other and then laughing as one backed off, saying, "You first," and the other would reply, "No, go ahead."

Caleb offered several suggestions, but Jeb could not help noticing that Faith was very quiet. She watched her mother as if Megan were a stranger. It was certain that Megan's vibrancy and confidence were new to the girl. Cindy was eager to please, volunteering for any assignment, especially those that would have her working with Faith. The younger girl clearly thought the sun rose and set in Faith Osbourne. Jeb had been glad to see that, if Faith were aware of this hero worship, she did nothing to take advantage of it. Instead she treated Cindy more like a younger sister. She was protective, occasionally interrupting the chatter of the others to ask Cindy what she thought.

In an hour as they sat around Reba's kitchen table devouring hamburgers from the grill, Reba's fried potatoes and a salad of early garden greens, they laid out an impressive plan for the center. Caleb excused himself to get started on the drive home to Milwaukee, and promised to text Jeb if he came up with any additional ideas. The young couple walked hand in hand out to Caleb's car, and Megan nervously began clearing the table, talking excitedly to cover the sudden silence outside. Jeb saw Cindy give her mother a sly look and pucker her lips as she glanced out the screen door.

"Come on, pumpkin," Jessica said, hugging Cindy close. "Let's head home—you've got school tomorrow." She stood at the open door to call out her goodbyes and immediately they all heard the engine of Caleb's car fire.

"Thank you," Jeb heard Megan whisper as she walked Jessica and Cindy out to the porch. He realized that Jessica had deliberately interrupted an excessively long farewell that Faith and Caleb might be engaged in. And when he saw tears brimming on Faith's lashes as she ran past them all and into the bathroom, he knew Jessica had guessed right.

When Megan went off to comfort Faith, Jeb finished packing his books and clothes he'd brought to the inn, and moved back up to the parsonage. Later that night he stood at the sink in the small kitchen and looked down at the inn. Lights glowed in the upstairs windows where guests were staying. The porch light was on, making Jeb smile.

"That advertising line about leaving a light on for you?" Reba had huffed one morning at breakfast after reprimanding him for turning out the porch light the night before. "That was my Stan's motto. 'How will folks know to stop if there's no light?' he used to ask."

Jeb knew that the light over the stove in the large country kitchen also stayed on through the night. "You never know when a body might need a cold glass of milk or something to eat," Reba had told him.

The truth was he was going to miss staying at the inn. The parsonage certainly had everything he needed, but it felt lifeless compared to the inn. He shut off the kitchen light and walked down the narrow hall to the front of the house. He paused at the door of the living room, crowded with the somber, heavy furniture Reverend Dunhill and his wife seemed to have preferred.

He stood there for a moment, thinking about the role of a parsonage in a ministry. It wasn't just where the preacher and his family lived. It set the tone for the kind of ministry the congregation might expect. According to most reports, Dunhill had preferred heavy-handed sobriety in his messages and lifestyle. But that had never been Jeb's style. He was a people person and that trait had been at the core of the success he'd achieved in the corporate world. Now he was in a new profession but he'd discovered that some things were not so different. When you got right down to it, the role of spiritual leader had a lot in common with the job of CEO in a large company.

Jeb retraced his steps and sat down at the dining-room table that served as his home office. He started to make notes. *God, CEO for the World,* he wrote at the top of a yellow legal pad. Yep, it would make a good topic for a sermon.

* * *

Megan and Jessica continued to bounce new ideas off one another. Sometimes it was over tea while Megan prepared breakfast for the inn's guests and sometimes it was later in the day over mugs of steaming coffee at the Shack.

"By Jove, I think we've got it," Jessica said late in the afternoon a week later, mimicking a British accent. "Why don't you have Faith e-mail Caleb tonight to fill him in on the final plans. We need his buy-in for the grand opening, when he and his family come up next week for the summer."

Megan frowned. "I'm not sure Faith has been in contact with Caleb lately."

"Trouble in teen paradise?"

"I think she expected to get an invitation to his graduation. Not that I would have let her go. Still, the gesture would have meant something." Megan closed the binder where she kept copious notes on plans for the youth center. "I'll e-mail the whole committee tonight. I need to catch up on some work on the computer at the inn."

They each took a sip of their coffee.

"How are things with you and Jeb?" Jessica asked, eyeing Megan over the rim of her mug.

"I… We… That is…" Megan sputtered, searching for some possible response to such a ridiculous question.

Jessica laughed. "Oh, honey, I do wish you could see your face."

"I don't know what you mean," Megan said irritably.

"Yes, you do," Jessica said, her tone gentle and caring. "You like him. He clearly likes you. Is there an issue I don't see?"

"We're friends."

"Come on, Meggie, this is me you're talking to. We may have been out of touch, so to speak, but we know each other better than most sisters do."

Megan seized on the opportunity to change the subject even if it meant talking about something that could be potentially painful or even damaging for their renewed friendship. "I've been meaning to tell you how much I regret all the time that we've wasted. I mean, now that I realize what we might have had in spite of…"

"Okay, you want to talk about Danny? Let's talk."

The last thing she wanted to do was talk about Jessica's brother, but given a choice between that and Jessica's speculations about her growing attraction to Jeb, Megan chose Danny. "How is he?" she asked softly.

"He's the same—self-absorbed, arrogant and insecure." Jessica sighed. "I love him to death, but he's so tied to material things as marks of, not only his success, but who he is. More so since his last divorce. And he hardly ever sees his kids. I just wish…"

Her voice trailed off and Megan realized her friend was close to tears. "Jess, it's okay."

"No. It's not. I hate seeing him like this—so lost. He never comes home anymore, not since our folks died. Dad's funeral in Milwaukee was the last time, and then he flew in that morning and back that very night."

It was odd to be comforting Jessica about a boy— now a man—who had abandoned Megan in her hour of need and never once acknowledged Faith. Shouldn't she be feeling some small satisfaction that he appeared to be unhappy? That maybe the life of fame and fortune he'd been set on hadn't turned out so well after all? But all she felt was sympathy for her friend, crying in earnest now.

"I'm sorry," Jessica blubbered, wiping tears away with the cuff of her flannel shirt. "You of all people…sorry."

"Now, you listen to me, Jessica Burbank," Megan said, leaning closer as she held her friend's hand across the table. "Danny made his choices and I made mine. My only concern was, is and always will be that Faith not be hurt."

"Don't you think it hurts to know your father abandoned you?" Jessica shot back, and then her face crumpled anew. "Oh, Meggie, I'm sorry. I wasn't thinking."

"My mother made her choice," Megan said softly. "And just like Faith knows where Danny is, I know my mother is out there and if I wanted to I could find her, confront her, spew out all the pain and grief she caused in my life." Megan shrugged. "And exactly what would that accomplish? If someone doesn't want you, doesn't want to be with you, Jess, all you can do is understand that it's that person's choice. It may not be yours, but there's very little you can do to change it. You just have to go on with the life God gave you and maybe hope that one day that other person might reconsider."

"How can you have that much forgiveness in you?" Jess whispered.

"It's easy to forgive others," Megan said. "It's forgiving yourself that comes hard."

"No wonder Jeb Matthews looks at you sometimes the way he does. You have preacher's wife written all over you, girl!"

Megan burst out laughing. This was the Jessica she knew and loved, the friend who would follow her down any detour from the initial topic but would find a way to tie it all back to that uncomfortable original question. "Reba is one matchmaker too many in my life, Jess.

Don't you start, too." She gathered her things. "Have to run. I'll e-mail everyone."

"Hey, Meggie?"

Megan turned and smiled.

"Good to be back to normal, don't you think? I've missed 'us.'"

"Yeah. Me, too."

Jeb stood off to one side of the renovated church basement hall. The place was packed with young people and their parents. It was hard to believe that this light, spacious room was the same dank and gloomy place it had been just a week earlier. One afternoon Pete Burbank had arrived with a crew of local teens and their parents. In short order and under the watchful eye and drill-sergeant direction of Jessica, they had scrubbed and painted walls, cleaned and replaced windows, changed light fixtures and installed a new tile floor.

Then Megan had driven up the hill, leading a caravan of minivans and pickup trucks loaded with furnishings she'd persuaded merchants as far away as Eagle River to donate to the cause. New lounge chairs, a sofa, half a dozen café sets, bookcases and magazine racks, even a flat-screen television. Next she unloaded plastic bins filled with dishes, utensils, throw pillows, books and pictures to complete the décor.

"Everyone has been so incredibly generous," she'd gushed, wide-eyed with wonder as if she hadn't had a thing to do with moving people toward that generosity. "I mean, look at this."

Thinking about it now, Jeb couldn't help remembering how beautiful she'd looked despite her oversize coveralls and the paint-spattered newsboy cap that covered her hair. In her eyes he saw such pride and joy—not for herself, but in the deeds of others. And from that day he'd been drawn to her in a way that he had to admit was most decidedly not one of minister to parishioner.

Now he watched from across the transformed room as Megan proudly pointed to one item or another and told the history of the gift to a group of parents gathered around her. She was wearing a simple blue summer dress and white sandals and, as usual, her makeup was limited to a bit of lip gloss and mascara. What else did she need? Jeb thought.

"You're about as hard to read as she is," Jessica said, handing him an ice cream sundae and nodding in Megan's direction. "When are you going to stop dancing around each other and start a serious courtship?"

Jeb laughed and took a bite of his sundae. He liked Jessica and her husband. Pete was as quiet and reserved as Jessica was direct and outspoken. They fit each other perfectly. "Hey, I've barely been here a month."

Jessica's eyes narrowed. "Don't toy with her, Jeb. She's had a hard life."

"I wouldn't," Jeb protested, surprised to even be having this conversation.

"You wouldn't intentionally. But for a woman like Meggie with her history…well, you can't play by the usual rules."

"Understood," Jeb said and concentrated on his ice cream.

Jessica touched his shoulder. "Hey, I'm just a meddling friend—hopefully yours as well as Megan's. Don't pay any attention to me, or anyone else. Go with your heart. You'll be fine." Then she spotted one of her twins climbing a tall bookcase. "Robert Franklin

Burbank," she shouted, "get down from there this minute." And she was gone.

Jeb carried his empty dish to the pass-through window of the kitchen. Megan was at the sink now, washing dishes and humming softly to herself.

"Hey there," Jeb said. "Great work getting this place up and running. I think we've got a hit on our hands."

She was beaming. "The kids seem to really like it," she said. "Jessica and Pete have worked wonders with the place and the kids—I mean, Faith and Cindy and even Caleb…"

"Caleb has his talents," Jeb said, stepping into the kitchen and picking up a dish towel.

"I know he does. He's really a leader among the teen crowd and his family—well, they've been coming up for summers for so long they're practically considered locals." She handed him a plate to dry and turned to put another stack in the soapy water.

"But you worry about his intentions toward Faith," Jeb said.

"Actually, I have little doubt about his intentions. I worry about how Faith might interpret his sudden attention to her. I mean, he's barely left her side all evening. I guess I thought when he came back for the summer and the other, older summer kids were also here he'd be less inclined…"

"Haven't you noticed? Since he got back Faith has barely given the poor guy the time of day. Caleb isn't used to being ignored."

Megan smiled. "Yeah. I'm pretty proud of the way Faith has handled herself. She was really disappointed that once he returned to Milwaukee she barely heard from him."

"She'll be fine," Jeb said. "She's had a very good teacher—two great teachers, if you count Reba."

He saw a flicker of doubt cloud Megan's eyes. "I just want so much for her."

"Do you ever think about wanting for yourself, Megan?"

She looked up at him. "What could I possibly want? I've already been so blessed. I have Reba and Faith, work I enjoy in a community I love, and all of this in spite of…well, let's just say it didn't always seem like things would turn out so well for me—for Faith and me."

She handed him the last bowl and he wiped it and spread the towel on the counter to dry. "Want to get some air?" he asked. "It's the first really warm night we've had since I got here."

Her hesitation was brief but undeniable.

"I'd really like to take off the preacher face for a bit and just enjoy the evening, Megan," he added.

She looked up at him, her eyes scanning his features. "I wasn't aware you had a 'preacher' face," she said.

"Oh, sure. I actually have an entire wardrobe of them." He pulled an exaggerated expression of deep concern and sympathy then immediately switched to a deeply furrowed brow and the scowl of disapproval. "And the one that always seems to work," he said, folding his hands piously in front of him and looking down at her with a benign smile.

"Stop that." She was laughing though. "Let me just get my sweater. I left it upstairs and…"

"No need," he said, removing his suit jacket and placing it around her shoulders. "Got you covered."

"Jeb, I…" The doubt was back.

"Shh," he whispered. "It's two friends out for a walk on a summer night, nothing more, okay?"

But once they were outside Megan found that she was all too aware of the man walking beside her, his hands in his pockets as he breathed in the sweet scent of lilac and honeysuckle.

"I love lilac," he said. "To me it's one of God's best shots at creating the perfect flower. Think about it. It has color and fragrance and it bursts out of the bush like lavender fireworks, right about the time of year when we most need something so alive and abundant."

"It's my favorite flower, too," Megan said. "One time Reba's husband, Stan, surprised me by filling pots and pots with lilac branches and setting them in my room." She giggled at the memory. "I could barely open the door."

"It must have been a special occasion. Your birthday?"

"No. Stan always said sometimes you need to do special things just because it's a Tuesday or another perfectly ordinary day. He was like that—always thinking up ways to show his love."

"You must miss him."

"I do, but Reba's the one whose loss is greater. They were married for nearly fifty years. I don't know how women like Reba and Ginny Epstein get past a loss like that. I…" She covered her mouth in horror, remembering that Jeb had also lost his wife—and his child. "Oh, Jeb, I'm so sorry. Prattling on here and not even thinking of how painful this must be for you. I mean, your loss must still be so fresh and…"

They had walked down the hill from the church to the inn. The wide front porch, with its row of white wicker rocking chairs overlooking the lake across the road, was deserted. "Let's sit here for a while," Jeb said, indicating the porch.

He waited until she was seated in a rocker and then he sat on the top step of the porch looking up at her, his face in shadow while hers was highlighted by the full moon above the calm lake waters.

"I'd like to tell you about that, Megan—the deaths of my wife and daughter. I've never really told anyone the entire story, but you've been through your share of grief and pain. I've realized that I need to talk about this to someone, and something tells me that you'll have a special understanding because you've experienced a similar loss."

"I'm listening."

Chapter Eight

Jeb ran his hands through his hair and then stared out at the lake, where the moon shot a spotlight across the still waters. "The facts are pretty basic—not that unique. Deborah took our daughter, Sally, to see a movie one night. It was winter and rain was turning to sleet by the time they left the theater. For whatever reason, instead of taking the expressway to our suburb, she decided to drive the back roads—roads she was unfamiliar with in daylight. Roads that can narrow suddenly and wind their way through the landscape."

He was aware only of the stillness that surrounded him. Megan had not moved since he'd begun talking. He turned slightly to look back at her. She was sitting forward in the chair, her hands clasped in her lap. He couldn't see her face, but she radiated empathy and concern.

"The officer who first arrived on the scene believed that she missed a turn, skidded on the slippery pavement and lost control. He also mentioned that she had to be doing at least seventy, and that…" He swallowed hard forcing out the one detail he had never admitted aloud.

"That made me wonder," he said, his voice almost a whisper. He cleared his throat and continued. "You see, the reason she'd left with Sally for the movies is that we had had a terrible argument. We'd been arguing for weeks, but this one was different. This time each of us said things that we knew would be hard to take back. This was the first time we'd actually used the word *divorce,* and it was all anger with no attempt on either of our parts to see the other side of things."

"Oh, Jeb, you can't think that your wife deliberately…I mean, she had your daughter in the car."

"No. She would never intentionally harm Sally. She was just so furious. I had never seen that level of rage in her before. If only…" A shudder racked his body and then Megan was sitting on the step next to him, one palm resting gently on his back. The gesture was so spontaneous, so filled with genuine understanding that Jeb felt the loosening of bonds of doubt and guilt he'd carried with him since that terrible day.

Megan continued to sit with him, rubbing his back in a rhythmic pattern and letting him cry. Finally she said, "You know I was so young when my mother left us. But the older I got the more I used to wonder about her leaving. What could Dad have done to make her stay? Or worse, had it been my fault? Was it because of me that she decided to leave?"

"You weren't responsible. You were a child, an innocent," Jeb said, regaining control of his emotions as the focus shifted to Megan.

"And neither were you. Your wife had had time to calm down while she was at the movies. You mentioned that it was late and the rain had made the road slippery."

"But she never took that road."

"What if she took it thinking it was a shortcut? What if she wanted so much to get home to you and put things right that she took a risk?"

"I never thought of it that way—I was always thinking about the way we'd left things." He looked out over the water. "Thanks. That helps more than you know."

"I'm so sorry you had to go through this. Losing a child…well, it's beyond comprehension."

"Yeah."

There didn't seem to be anything else to say so they sat there for a long moment, listening to the night sounds, thinking their own thoughts.

"Megan?"

"Right here," she joked, thinking perhaps it was time to lighten the mood a bit.

"How could you think that you had anything to do with your mother's leaving?"

He felt her shoulder brush his as she shifted. "I felt that way for a long time—until Faith was born, really. And then I realized that in so many ways my life was much more difficult than my mother's was. She had a husband. I had an entire town that chose to believe I had gotten myself knocked up by some stranger, rather than face the fact that their hometown hero might have feet of clay. She had a home and the financial means to raise me in style. I had a father who lost all of that when he chose the bottle over raising me. And I had the welfare system always threatening foster care, but never really getting around to it since we lived out here in the boondocks."

Jeb turned so that he was looking directly at her. He took her hands, stroking the backs of her fingers with his thumb. "You had Reba and Stan, and you had Faith," he said.

"She became my life and the more I loved her, the more I understood that Mom not loving me enough to stay or take me with her was her problem. It was not something I had done or not done. She made a choice." She linked her fingers with his. "And Jeb, your wife may or may not have had a choice that night but if she did, then it was her choice."

Jeb had long been aware that healing could come from many sources—prayer, time, new life directions— but it had never occurred to him that the very words he needed most to hear would come from this woman who'd had a life filled with struggle and disappointment. "You're an incredibly perceptive woman, Megan Osbourne," he said, his voice husky with admiration.

As he'd learned was her way, she brushed off the compliment. "Naw—I've just had more time to come to terms with my losses than you have with yours. And really, there's no comparison. I mean, I don't know what I was thinking. Your wife and child died. My mother is still out there somewhere—probably."

"You don't know for sure?"

"When I was in high school I stopped looking. You know teenagers. I was in my if-you-don't-want-me-then-I-don't-need-you period. And then shortly after that I realized I was pregnant and, well, I had bigger things to think about than whether or not I was ever going to see my mother again."

"And now that Faith is almost grown and will soon be off to college?"

Megan laughed nervously. "Let's not wish time away, Jeb. She still has a year of high school and, as for college—well, we'll see. Besides how did this suddenly become all about me?"

"Because you're fascinating," Jeb said, his tone completely serious. "I've never met anyone like you, Megan. I was serious when I told you that if you'd have come in for a job at my company I would have hired you on the spot."

"With no qualifications?" She was trying to turn the compliment into a joke.

Jeb tightened his hold on her hands and leaned toward her. "People lie on résumés all the time, Megan. I long ago developed the skill to see through the listed credentials—or lack of them. You have life skills and innate intelligence that a Harvard graduate would envy. But I'm no longer interested in hiring you."

Her breath caught and she tried to pull away, but Jeb hung on.

"What I'm saying, Megan, is that I don't know what God has in mind for us, but I know for sure that He brought us together for a reason. It may be that we're destined to be the best of friends. It may be something more. Right now I'm hoping it's that 'something more.' How about you?"

She tried speaking, but no sound came out, so she nodded.

Jeb's grin exploded across his face. He couldn't remember a time in recent years when he had felt more pure joy. "I'm going to kiss you now, Megan," he announced. "Purely for research, you understand."

To his surprise, Megan straightened her back and lifted her chin. Her face was bathed in moonlight and she had closed her eyes and was waiting. She was the picture of innocence and trust. Jeb placed his palms on her cheeks and drew her to him. He kissed her gently, allowing time to appreciate the full softness of her lips, but releasing her before the kiss could move to the next level.

Instead of pulling away she rested her forehead against his. "Jeb?"

"Hmm?"

"No strings, okay? Friendship is such a precious gift and, well, I don't want to mess that up."

"Let's just trust God's way for us and see where it leads," he said and kissed her once more.

Megan felt as if she could play the role of Eliza Doolittle in *My Fair Lady*. She might not sing as well as a Broadway actress, but ever since Jeb had kissed her she definitely could have danced all night. In the two days that had passed since the opening of the youth center, she had hardly been able to contain her happiness. And every time she ran into Jeb—at the market and then later, when he stopped by to bring Reba a gift certificate for her favorite bookstore as a way of thanking her for taking him in—she couldn't seem to stop smiling. She might have known that a kiss would change things between them and it had, but not in the way she had thought. Instead of being shy and uncertain with him, she found herself flirting and teasing him. The way he looked at her with that slightly crooked smile set her heart racing. And tonight, she thought as she and Reba worked together on the week's laundry, they were going to Eagle River for dinner and a movie. A date— an actual date.

"You've changed," Reba announced.

Megan felt a flush rise along her neck and cheeks. While she and Jeb had had eyes only for each other these last couple of days, she had forgotten that others had eyes on them. "How?" she asked, swallowing the protest that would have been a lie.

Reba squinted her eyes. "Can't put my finger on it. Just kind of giddy—silly almost. Now if it was Faith acting that way, I'd understand. She has got a case of the fever for that city boy for sure, in spite of the fact that she's trying not to show it."

Megan unloaded the dryer, then started moving heavy wet linens from the washer to the dryer. "Faith's too smart to think Caleb's attention is anything more than a summer fling." But she didn't sound convinced and her mood was suddenly as heavy as the sodden laundry she was lifting.

"Whatever. We're not talking about Faith anyway. We're talking about you, missy. Your change couldn't have something to do with a certain young minister, could it?"

Reba's comment about Faith had not only dampened Megan's mood, it had made her downright irritable. "His name is Jeb, Reba, and we're friends. We find we have a lot in common, strange as that may seem, with him being a former big-time business executive and my barely making it through high school." She slammed the dryer door and started preparing her and Faith's clothes for a personal load.

"Oh, honey, why do you put yourself down that way? You were top of your class and everyone knows it. The fact that the school board was too provincial to let a pregnant girl deliver the valedictory address is hardly something you need to take on yourself. No matter. You landed well and that's the test of it."

Megan started to speak, but Reba wasn't finished.

"And," she continued, holding up her palm like a

stop sign, "Jeb Matthews sees your inner as well as outer beauty, and he appreciates your brain, which is long overdue for the chance to show what it can do, and that just proves the point. Why, Nellie Barnsworth stopped me at the post office this morning and started singing your praises."

"I doubt that," Megan said.

"Okay. She was trying to pump me for information about how you and Jeb were getting on. I told her that as far as I knew you were working together—with Jessica Burbank and others—to make the youth center a success. And that's when she said that… What is it, honey? Sit down a minute. You're white as this sheet."

Reba directed Megan onto the stool and hovered over her, testing for fever with the back of her hand, cupping Megan's chin with the other. "Talk to me," she ordered, her voice husky with concern.

Megan allowed Faith's jeans that she'd been holding to slide to the floor and held up a small metal object. "This was in Faith's pocket," she said. "It's a bottle cap, Reba. From a beer bottle." This last came in a whisper.

"I'm sure…" Reba began, but her expression told Megan she wasn't sure at all.

"It's Caleb." Megan pushed herself off the stool and headed for the door, but Reba blocked her way.

"Now, just hold your horses. Think before you go and make matters worse. You found a bottle cap. There could be half a dozen explanations of how that ended up in her pocket. You go charging off the way you are now, you'll do nothing but drive those two young people closer. Take a breath and think."

But when it came to alcohol and the damage it could do, Megan was incapable of rational thought. The years she had spent putting her father to bed after he came home drunk, living with his promises to give it up, watching his health decline, were all too vivid. Megan's hatred and fear for what alcohol could do knew no bounds.

On the other hand, Reba was a force to be reckoned with when she needed to be—and this was one of those times. Short of knocking the older woman aside, Megan had little choice but to back away.

And then she heard Faith call from the front hallway. "Mom?" She sounded upset, and this time Reba stepped aside voluntarily as both women hurried into the front lobby.

"What's happened?" Reba asked, her eyes searching Faith for possible physical injury.

But Faith strode past Reba as if she weren't even there and faced her mother. "Is it true? Are you and the preacher seeing each other? It's the talk of the town and everyone is saying…" Her face contorted with horror. "You aren't…lovers, are you?"

Megan clenched her fist to restrain herself from striking her beloved child. She squeezed her eyes shut and sent up a silent prayer for patience and wisdom. "Lower your voice, Faith. This is a place of business."

Faith just continued to glare at her. "Well?"

"We'll discuss this later at home," Megan told her. To her shock, Faith burst into angry tears and stormed off into the kitchen, where she started unloading the dishwasher—one of her regular afternoon chores. Only this time each dish was slammed into its place in the cupboard, and cabinet doors crashed against each other.

"You don't get it, do you?" Faith shouted. Megan had followed her and Reba had closed the door to the kitchen and remained at the front desk. "I have spent my whole life being better than the best because I was the girl who didn't have a father—who didn't even know for sure who Daddy was, and now you've set your sights on the minister? Do you know what people are saying? Do you know that they think you're chasing after Reverend Matthews and he's being nice because he feels sorry for you? You're a laughingstock, Mom, and furthermore, you're making me one, as well."

"Calm down and lower your voice, young lady," Megan instructed, surrendering to the inevitability of holding this conversation now. She felt the imprint of the bottle cap on her clenched palm. "Reverend Matthews and I are friends," she began, but could not deny that Faith's words had stung. More to the point they had brought to the surface doubts and insecurities that Megan had thought were not issues. "It's true that he asked me out for dinner and a movie tonight, but that can wait. You and I need to talk, Faith, and not just about my friendship with Jeb." She picked up the receiver of the wall phone and punched Reba's code for the church office.

"Hey there." Jeb's voice was like salve on a raw sore. She knew he'd seen the inn's number on caller ID. He was probably thinking Reba was calling.

"Hi," she said and cleared her throat. "It's me."

She was as sure of his smile as if he were the one standing not two feet away, instead of her red-faced, scowling daughter.

"Hi, me," he teased. "Couldn't wait to see me, huh?"

Ordinarily Megan would have fired back with some joke about him not being so sure of himself. Instead she cut to the chase. "I'm going to have to cancel. Something's come up."

"Reba?" His tone was professional, concerned.

"No. A family matter."

"Faith?" He was clearly surprised, as anyone who knew the girl would have been. Faith was never a problem, never one to cause concern, never… "She's all right, isn't she?"

Megan heard the edge of panic in the question. "She's fine. We just need— A couple of things came up suddenly today that we need to work through."

"Can I help?"

"I'll let you know."

"Rain check then on tonight?"

Megan hesitated. "I'll let you know," she murmured.

"Megan?"

She slipped the receiver back into its cradle and faced her child. In the silence between them the dryer buzzer shrilled. "Finish your chores," Megan said. "I'm going to get that last load of laundry started and then we'll go up to the house and talk about things."

"Things?" Faith's tone dripped with sarcasm.

Megan hesitated only a moment before retracing her steps and placing the beer bottle cap squarely in the center of the empty kitchen table. "Things," she said, forcing in her voice a calm and steadiness she was far from feeling.

Jeb kept an eye on Reba's small house while he washed up his supper dishes. After Megan's phone call, he'd seen her and Faith walk up the hill to the house and go inside. Their body language told the story. Faith lagged behind Megan's purposeful strides across the lawn. Megan's head was bent while Faith's chin jutted forward defiantly, and Jeb couldn't help thinking that if his own daughter had lived, there would surely have been moments like this between them.

Several hours had passed since he'd observed that scene and now he was wondering if he should call Megan. Just check in to be sure everything was all right. He was about to retrieve his cell phone from his desk when he saw Reba's back porch light go on. Then he watched as Reba shooed Megan out the kitchen door. He heard the two women exchange comments but could not make them out. Megan stood on the porch for a minute, looking around as if lost, then started down the driveway.

Jeb grabbed a light jacket—more for Megan than himself—and followed her. She stopped at the roadside to wait for passing traffic and then crossed over to the inn's small beach and pier on the lake. He was halfway down the hill when he stopped, his role as Megan's minister warring with his deep personal attraction to her.

His training dictated that he be available to those he served, but not intrusive. "If a person is not ready to hear what you have to say," one professor had advised, "you cannot change that. You can only let them know you are there and wait for that person to turn to you—and to God."

On the other hand this woman, who he had come to care for in a way he had thought impossible, was clearly in pain. He watched as she stood at the end of the pier, her fists clenched at her sides, her face raised to the darkening skies, her body rigid. She was a portrait in loneliness and, when he saw her shoulders sag, her arms wrapped around herself as if trying to keep from flying apart as she knelt on the pier, Jeb's decision was made.

"It's getting cooler," he said softly, as he draped the jacket over her shoulders and then sat on the pier next to her without touching her further. She'd been sobbing when he'd reached her, her tears raining unchecked down her cheeks, her breath coming in choked gasps.

Jeb picked up a small smooth rock from a collection someone had left on the pier and skipped the stone across the water. Then another and another until all of them were gone. As the last stone sank, sending out rings of ripples on the water that spread all the way back to where they sat, Megan pulled his jacket tighter around her and let go the last of her tears with a sigh.

"I always thought that Dad might teach me how to do that—skip stones like that," she said. Her voice was wistful as if coming from far away. "Then I could have taught Faith. There were so many things I never taught her—things a father probably would have."

"Skipping stones might be overrated on the scale of things you need to teach a child," Jeb said.

"Maybe. Lying isn't overrated though."

"You think Faith is lying to you? About what?"

"Earlier today I found a cap from a beer bottle in the pocket of her jeans. When I confronted her about it, she said it was just a good luck piece that Caleb gave her."

"And you think?"

"I think that the reason Caleb gave her the cap was to commemorate her first taste of beer."

Jeb thought she was probably right and wondered if he had ever taken the time to be so perceptive when it had come to his daughter, Sally.

"That's just half the story." Megan glanced at him and then immediately back at the dark water below. "Faith is upset about—well, us. She claims we are quite the topic of gossip around town these days, especially in her peer group."

Jeb suppressed a smile. "Hey, that's just kids. Their hormones are raging and they can't imagine that's not true for any man and woman who happen to spend time together."

"I have lived in this town my whole life, Jeb. And for most of that life I have been a topic of gossip. Faith and I had just reached a place in our lives where it seemed like people were willing to accept us as we are."

"And you believe that our spending time together has somehow jeopardized that?" For the second time that evening a minister's objectivity struggled with a man's personal feelings—and lost. "You can't let kids dictate your life, Megan."

"Faith is my life."

Jeb closed his eyes, silently praying for words that would offer her the counsel she needed without being complicated by his own needs. "Have you thought about a day, Megan, when you will have launched Faith into a life of her own? When the best you can do for her is to let her go?"

"All the time," she admitted. "I just didn't think it would come so fast."

"You have to trust in the tools you've given her to make the right decisions. She'll be tested in many ways and she might even yield to temptation, as you suspect she did in tasting beer. But in the long run…"

"Oh, Jeb, don't you see that the beer is more than just a run-of-the-mill temptation? My father—her grandfather—is an alcoholic. He has tried probably hundreds of times to quit, or rationalize his ability to stop at one drink, and failed. I am so afraid for Faith. If it had been anything else…"

And suddenly Jeb understood that because of her

fear that Faith might get pulled under by a family history of alcohol, Megan was willing to do anything.

"Megan, when you first got down here to the pier, it looked like you might be praying. Were you making a bargain with God?"

Chapter Nine

Megan felt her back arch like a cat preparing for a fight. "I know it may seem childish to you, Jeb, but offering God something in exchange for His help works for me. I don't believe someone like me…"

"Stop right there," Jeb said. "God doesn't pick and choose, Megan. All prayers are equal."

"Okay, poor choice of words. What I'm trying to say is… Oh, I can't explain it to you. Can't you just respect that offering something in return for a blessing works for me?"

"How?"

"When Faith was born I promised God that if He would help me I would dedicate myself to making sure she had a good life. There were some in town who wanted me to give her up for adoption. There was a summer couple who had been unable to have children who were willing to pay for me to go to college in exchange for giving up all claim to Faith."

"Didn't you see that as God offering you a way to assure Faith's future—and your own?"

"But how could I know that for sure? What if that couple divorced and Faith was miserable? What if she believed I had abandoned her just so that I could have the life I wanted?"

"Is that why you think your mother left?"

"I don't know why she left and probably never will. I didn't want that uncertainty for my child. And when Reba offered to take us in, that felt like God's true answer."

"So tonight the bargain was what?"

Megan felt a shyness wash over her. "This is going to sound ridiculous," she warned.

"Try me."

"It's not you—not really. Now that I think about it, anytime Faith thought I was getting involved with someone, she shut down or acted out. I understand that it was her dislike of change. Before Reba took us in, there were some hard years with her grandfather. She adored him, but he could appear to love her in return one day and be unspeakably cruel to her the next. And that doesn't begin to address the questions she was having about her own father abandoning her."

"But she had Reba's husband, Stan."

"And he was wonderful with her, but his death came suddenly and unexpectedly and I think probably added to the evidence she was building that men cannot be counted upon. She was inconsolable for months afterward." She turned to him. "I wish you had been here then, Jeb. Reverend Dunhill was a good man, but his answer to most tragedy was that it was 'God's will.' For a child, that's slim comfort."

"For anyone," Jeb murmured. He cleared his throat. "So it was just Reba, Faith and you."

Megan nodded. "For years now that's been the way of it. Faith calls us the Cranberry Hill Trio."

"And you think she's afraid that if you and I…"

"Oh, Jeb, it would be anyone—could even be a woman that she saw as disturbing the safe cocoon she's built for herself. And as you say, in another year she'll be off to college and on her way to the life God's planned for her as an adult." She placed her hand on Jeb's. "It's a year, Jeb, and in the meantime, we can still work together on church and community things and…"

"That's the bargain? You put us on hold in exchange for what?"

"Helping Faith fight whatever temptations Caleb and his crowd might send her way," Megan admitted.

"And what if God has other plans—for Faith and for you?"

She shrugged. "Then He'll make that clear in time. In the meantime, I'll stick to my promise."

"To stop seeing me?"

"To not see you socially in a way that drives my daughter away from me," Megan corrected. "Besides, Jeb, you've just moved here and I was one of the first people you met. We got thrown together when Henry died and then again working on the youth center and…"

Jeb hooked a finger under her chin, forcing her to look at him through the darkness. "Hey, I'm not interested in shopping around. I never thought that I would be drawn to another woman once my wife died. And then I met you and, I'm not going to lie to you, the attraction was instant and undeniable. I don't know what you felt, but I am well aware of what I felt. Here's my bargain—I'll give you the time you need if you allow me to be part of your life on some level—one that includes the opportunity for me to show Faith that I can be a refuge rather than a threat."

Megan was suddenly overcome by a sense of lightness and peace that sharply contrasted the heaviness in her heart that had brought her to the pier earlier. And in that spirit she went with her heart. "Thank you," she whispered as she hugged Jeb. She felt that the words were meant for Jeb because he understood, and at the same time were offered up as a prayer for God's blessing in sending her this dear man.

On her way to her room, Megan paused outside Faith's door for a long moment. They had had strong words before Faith had stormed upstairs, and Megan had gone to the pier. One of Reba's house rules was that no one goes to bed with hard feelings still unresolved. Megan tapped lightly at Faith's door and then entered her daughter's bedroom.

Faith was lying on her side under the covers, but her very stillness told Megan she was not asleep. The small lamp on the bedside table was still on. Megan sat on the side of the bed and stroked her daughter's fine golden hair. "Early for you to be in bed," she said, making sure there wasn't an ounce of criticism in her tone. "Could we talk some more?"

Faith curled further into herself. "What's to talk about?"

"Oh, well, there are lots of things. Things like the fact that sometimes when I look at you and realize how fast you are growing up and how beautiful you are inside and outside, it scares me."

Faith's tension relaxed slightly and she half rolled toward Megan. "You're never scared," she said.

Megan laughed. "I put on a good act sometimes."

Faith turned onto her back and looked at Megan. "For me?"

"Sometimes."

"Why does my growing up scare you? Because you think I'll leave you and you'll be alone?"

"You would never do that, but it's also important that we both understand that you are on a journey to find your own life in this world. And as you move along that path, it's important that we both accept that I might make some changes, as well."

Faith's expression hardened. "Like marrying Reverend Matthews?"

"Oh, honey, Jeb and I have only known each other a short time. We're friends—mostly because we've both had some experiences that have been especially painful. It's unusual to find someone who truly understands that kind of sorrow, someone who isn't simply pretending to know."

"I know," Faith said softly. "Your mom left you the way my dad left me, so I know. The way Gramps abandoned both of us by drinking." Her eyes glistened with tears. "So I know. You can talk to me."

"Yes, you and I share a great deal, Faith, but you are my child and that colors everything. A friendship is different. You know that. Why, I'll bet there are any number of things—serious topics—that you can share with your girlfriends, and now Caleb, more easily than you could discuss them with me."

Faith chewed her lower lip, telling Megan that she was right. "Did Reverend Matthews—was he abandoned, too?"

"No. I think perhaps Jeb sees himself in the role of the one who abandoned his family, his wife and daughter."

"But they died in a car accident. That's what Mrs. Barnsworth said."

"And that's true, but it's not so simple as that. You of all people know that. When something like that happens a person always has questions. Could I have done something different that might have changed the course of events?"

"Yeah, I think about that." Faith laced her fingers with Megan's. "Mom? Why didn't Dad want us?"

It was the first time in years she had raised the question and Megan felt her heart constrict with the pain this dear child had carried with her all this time. "Oh, honey, I don't think it was so much not wanting us. He didn't even know you. If he had, that might have changed everything. But at the time I think your father must have been so scared. After all, we weren't much older than you are now. His whole world must have felt as if it was coming apart and he had so much to look forward to, so many people here in Singing Springs who wanted him to succeed."

"Didn't anybody stop to think your whole world might be coming apart, too?" Faith jutted her jaw—the mirror image of her father's stubborn jaw.

"Reba and Stan did, and there were others. Hey, things have turned out pretty well for you and me. You just need one person in your corner, Faith, and we've been more blessed than many."

Faith considered this. "So is that how you see Reverend Matthews? As someone who is in your corner?"

"Our corner," Megan corrected as she stood and tucked Faith in. "He's a good guy, honey."

"Yeah, I guess."

Megan leaned down and kissed Faith's forehead. "We're friends, Faith, nothing more, okay?"

Faith looked skeptical.

"Hey, we've got to trust each other, right? Isn't that what you told me earlier?" Actually, the girl had screamed it at her just before stomping up the stairs and slamming the door to her room. *How about trusting me, Mom?*

Megan had been halfway up the stairs herself when Reba had stopped her. "She's got a point, Meggie. There comes a time when you not only have to trust her, but also trust what you've taught her."

But she knew that at least part of the uncharacteristic overreaction to Megan's questions had arisen out of guilt. Faith was not telling her the whole story—about that beer bottle cap or about her relationship with Caleb. She brushed Faith's bangs away from her eyes.

"Now, get some sleep. Reba's got a full house moving in tomorrow." She switched off the lamp.

"Mom?"

"Yeah."

"I love you."

"I love you right back," Megan whispered, parroting the exchange she and Faith had developed when Faith was just a toddler. She closed the door softly behind her and stood for a moment in the hallway, basking in the realization that despite all her fears she had raised one terrific kid, wise and sensitive beyond her years. Faith would be all right.

As the days of June flew by, Jeb began to fully understand the dynamics of living in a town that seemingly overnight was teeming with tourists and summer residents. He saw one clear difference every Sunday morning as the pews of the old chapel gradually filled and he started to notice different faces from one week to the next. The youth center was also another indicator that things had changed. Every week there were new faces there, as well. And although he feared that the increase in traffic and work at the church might further restrict the already limited time he could spend with Megan, the opposite was true.

Several times a week Megan came to the church with baskets of fresh fruit donated by area farmers, baked treats still warm from the inn's oven, and books, DVDs and CDs donated by townspeople for the center's growing library of games, movies and what Reba liked to call "rainy day activities." On Sundays, Megan took her place next to Faith and Reba on the aisle in the third pew. And on weekday evenings when the center was open she was there, working side by side with Jessica in the church's tiny kitchen, serving up pizza or hot dogs or sometimes just sitting with a new visitor to the center.

"You can always tell the shy ones," she told him one night as he walked her home. "It's in the eyes—how much they long to be part of the group, to be cool. To be accepted."

"I can't imagine that you weren't ever part of the in-crowd," he teased and then immediately regretted the words. "I mean, before…" He shook off the rest of the explanation. "Sorry," he muttered.

"Don't be. You're right. When I was Faith's age and first started dating Danny Moreland, I thought I was the coolest kid in town. For the first time in my life I felt as if everyone was envious of me, when I had spent so many years being envious of any kid who had a real home life. It was heady stuff."

Jeb took her hand and she didn't resist. "And then?"

"Then I was pregnant and, well, if you force kids to

choose, they are going to go for self-preservation almost every time. Danny was the star. Without him I was hardly someone other kids looked up to or wanted to be like. Most of my friends felt they had to make a choice and it was kind of a no-brainer. I'd like to think I would have been more loyal to a friend than that, but when I'm honest with myself, I'm pretty sure I would have believed Danny and stuck by him."

"So now when you see a kid like that boy tonight?"

Megan shrugged. "I'm drawn to kids like that. I don't know whether it's because I want to warn them or reassure them, but I home in on them like a laser."

"And what do you say?"

"It varies. The key I think is to get the kid talking, draw him or her out, get a smile going. Then sometimes I'll call Faith over and she pretty much takes it from there. She's a natural when it comes to nurturing others."

"She's inherited that from her mother." They had reached Reba's back door, but Jeb was reluctant to let Megan go just yet. "Things seem to be better between the two of you."

They had not talked about that night on the pier, but as soon as the following day Jeb had seen a closeness between Megan and Faith that made his heart fill with the realization that he was never to have that with Sally. No, he had allowed that opportunity to pass him by, put it off for "someday." And that lesson learned in the most horrific way made it hard to keep his promise to Megan. Jeb was all too aware that "someday" had a way of never showing up.

"I still have my concerns when it comes to the amount of time she's spending with Caleb," Megan admitted, "especially now that his friends are here, too.

But you and Reba are right—I know that all I can do is be there for her and hope the lessons I've tried to instill over the years stick."

Jeb pulled her into his arms and held her. "She'll be fine. She's strong and smart and has great instincts—like her mom."

Megan rested her cheek against his chest with her arms wrapped around his waist. "Thanks, Rev Jeb." It was the nickname that Caleb had given him and it had stuck, serving to make him more approachable for the young people who now flocked to the center.

He kissed the top of her head. "See you tomorrow?"

She laughed and leaned away from him without breaking the hold. The amber glow of the porch lamp lit her face like candlelight. His heartbeat quickened. This wasn't just that feeling of pure joy he felt every time she entered a room or he heard her laughter. This was something deeper…unsettling and yet at the same time the moment brought him such a sense of peace. And as her smile faded to an expression of puzzlement, Jeb understood that Megan shared his feelings.

"Tomorrow," he said, kissing her forehead and releasing her. He started back up the hill to the parsonage and heard her open the back door. "We need to get the kids started on planning the parade entry for the Fourth," he called.

"Faith and Cindy already have an idea," she answered.

He turned and walked backward, mostly so he could see her one more time. "Does it involve my wearing a costume?"

Megan's laugh sang across the darkness like a wind chime. "Yeah. Faith said something about needing an Uncle Sam—on stilts."

Jeb stumbled on a tree root and lost his balance.

"Jeb," Megan shrieked and started toward him.

Jeb held up his hand to let her know he was fine and got to his feet. "Might want to rethink that stilts thing," he called. "Rev Jeb is apparently not the world's most coordinated guy."

"You're sure you're not hurt?"

"Only my pride. 'Night, Megan." He waved and waited until she went inside, then limped back to the parsonage. That ankle was going to need ice.

Life had settled back into a routine that Megan found comforting. Not only was her friendship with Jessica fully restored, but Faith was back to sharing her activities, thoughts and dreams for the future with her. More important, Megan was beginning to trust her growing feelings for Jeb. At night as she lay in bed saying her prayers, she often found herself thinking that maybe there could be a future for them. She had even started to dare hope that someday they might find their way to something beyond simple friendship. "Although friendship is gift enough," she assured God. "You have blessed my life in so many ways and I am so grateful," had become her nightly devotion.

After serving breakfast to the guests and helping Reba and Faith clean the rooms, she had walked into town to pick up the mail and stop by the Shack for what had become her daily morning coffee break with Jessica when she saw a man come out of the barbershop two blocks down. She paused as she always did on such occasions. There had been times since her father had left town when she'd thought she'd seen him. It had always turned out to be someone else and, with so many visitors in town, that was no doubt the case now. Yet there had been something…

"Hey there," Jessica called from the doorway of the Shack. "You gonna stand out there all day? I need coffee, girl, preferably intravenously. It has been a morning and it's not yet nine-thirty."

Megan grinned. "Don't mind me. Daydreaming," she said as she followed Jessica inside and stepped up to the self-serve coffee area. "Hey, you added a new flavor."

Jessica made a face. "Pete's idea. Pumpkin latte. He says it's like drinking warm pumpkin pie—not that I would ever want to do that, but to each his own. The usual or do you want to try this stuff?"

"Usual," Megan said, and she glanced up as someone passed the large window of the shop. She was having trouble shaking the image of the man entering the barbershop. On the other hand, one of the last places Owen Osbourne was likely to head if he returned to town was the barber's. More likely he would stop in at the tavern on the edge of town or the convenience store that sold beer.

"Speaking of daydreaming," Jessica said as she set the mug down on the table at the booth next to the window. They both slid across the worn red-vinyl seats. "How's things with you and Reverend Dreamboat?"

Megan blushed and Jessica laughed. "That good, huh?" she teased.

"We're just friends."

"Yeah, that's what he says, too. Well, you two keep on working with that premise if you feel you need to. But if you ask me you're wasting daylight. Life is short, sweetie, and why on earth would you willingly give up one hour, much less a day, week or more that you could be happy?"

"I am happy," Megan protested. "I have so much to be thankful for."

Jessica leaned back and studied Megan as she sipped her coffee. "Apples and oranges. Appreciating God's blessing does not necessarily equate with being happy. You never wanted anything for yourself, did you?"

"Only what I couldn't have," Megan said in the light-hearted tone of banter the two of them had always shared. Then, realizing how Jessica might take her words, she added, "I'm not talking about Danny, Jess."

Jessica waved aside her explanation. "I know that."

"Besides, I have so much. Faith is my life and…"

"Therein lies the problem," Jess said. "Kids leave, Meggie. What will your life be when she's off to college and a life of her own?"

"I'll be here with you and Reba and my friends, working and, well, I mean, it's not like Faith is going to just suddenly disappear one day like…" She stopped, shocked at what she had almost said.

"Like your mom, dad and Dan did?"

Megan forced a laugh. "Hey, it's too beautiful a day to be so maudlin. Talk about you. How are things going? The store looks busy." She glanced around at several customers browsing the racks and shelves of merchandise.

"Lookers mostly," Jessica said. "I was telling Pete just last night that we might want to think about getting into some other line of work." She ran a finger around the rim of her mug. "You don't think Reba would be interested in selling the inn one day, do you?"

"I… It hasn't come up…but…"

Megan stopped herself before she told Jessica that Reba's daughter in Arizona had been after Reba for some time now to sell or lease the inn and come to live with her—at least for the winters. Reba had made Megan promise not to breathe a word of such foolishness to anyone.

"She's getting up there," Jessica continued, "and her arthritis is obviously becoming a factor. I'm just saying if she ever mentions the idea, would you ask her to come talk to Pete and me before she does anything?" Jessica signaled she would be right back and got up to help a customer.

Megan took a swallow of her coffee, lukewarm now. She pushed the mug aside and turned to the window. What if Reba decided to sell? What if her daughter convinced her to leave Singing Springs?

Suddenly she was awash in images of Faith heading off to college and Reba to Arizona. The happiness she had felt an hour earlier might as well have been as much a figment of her imagination as the image of the man entering the barbershop.

Chapter Ten

Jeb had just sat down in the barber's chair when the bell over the door jangled and another man walked in. In the mirror Jeb saw surprise in Fred Hagen's eyes, but then he recovered. "Owen," Fred acknowledged as he finished fastening the plastic cape.

"Fred," the man replied.

"You're back?" he added a couple of minutes later as the scissors snipped their way through Jeb's thick hair.

The man had not moved, not picked up the newspaper, not shown much interest in anything except looking out the window.

"We'll see."

Jeb waited for Fred to make introductions, but the barber just frowned a little and concentrated on the haircut.

"Any work?" the man asked after several moments of silent tension that Jeb had not yet decided to break.

"Depends," Fred replied as he set the scissors aside and attached a trimmer to the electric razor. For a few seconds the buzz of the razor took precedence over conversation.

Fred shut off the razor and used a soft brush to clear away any stray hair on Jeb's neck. Then he unsnapped the apron and swept it away. The motion always reminded Jeb a little of a bullfighter and it had always made him smile. But his mind was on the stranger and the unusual aura that had permeated the small barbershop from the moment the man had arrived.

He offered the man a handshake. "Jeb Matthews," he said.

"Reverend Matthews," Fred muttered under his breath with a look at the stranger.

"Owen Osbourne." The man accepted the handshake and looked directly at Jeb for the first time.

The blue eyes were paler, older and wearier, but they were eyes he knew. They were Megan's eyes.

"Any relation to Megan Osbourne?" he asked, guessing the answer.

"I'm her father."

Jeb heard Fred issue a snort of derision and Owen turned on the barber. "You gonna pass judgment or cut my hair?"

Fred indicated the chair with a bow.

"Does Megan know you're in town?"

"Not yet. I thought I saw her headed out of the post office and over to the Shack. It's been a while," he added, as if that explained why he hadn't called out to her, followed her or somehow made his presence known.

Jeb was a little taken aback at the emotions warring within him. On the one hand, he felt such a strong surge of protectiveness for Megan that it nearly overwhelmed him. On the other, there was something about this man—a neediness, a sadness—that touched Jeb's innate need to offer comfort and solace.

"Would you like me to be with her when you see her the first time? I mean, I'm her pastor."

Owen's eyes narrowed with distrust. This was a man who had been burned before, badly enough that even a simple offer like this one was subject to doubt. "How about you let her know I'm in town and see what she wants to do?"

"All right," Jeb agreed. "But first I'd like to hear a little more of your reason for coming back at this particular time. What do you want from Megan?"

"She's my daughter," Owen growled.

"That's no answer, sir." Jeb handed Owen a card. "I'll be at the parsonage if you want to talk about the best way to let Megan know you're in town once you're finished here."

Owen took the card and glanced at it. "You took Dunhill's place?"

"He didn't take nobody's place," Fred growled. "He's his own man. Take my advice, Owen. Go talk to the man before you see Megan."

Owen tucked the business card in his shirt pocket and looked up at Jeb from under hooded lids, sizing him up. "I'll be up directly," he said, then glanced in the mirror. "Not so much off the top, Fred. There's little enough there to start."

Jeb nodded to Fred and left the shop. He stood for a moment on the sidewalk, wrestling with his choices. Should he go find Megan and alert her that her father was in town without waiting for him to come to the parsonage? Should he step across the street to the convenience store that also sold wine and beer and warn them about Owen's presence and his drinking history, in case he wandered in there for something to build up his courage?

He thought about what he'd observed of the man. He was clean, even if the clothing he wore was on the shabby side. Jeb had been close enough to the man in Fred's narrow, cramped space that he would know if Owen had been drinking recently. There had been no sign of that. His eyes had been a little rheumy, but not bloodshot or unfocused. His stride when he'd entered the shop had been hesitant rather than unsteady. And perhaps the most telling thing of all was the fact that Fred had simply accepted Owen's presence as a given, almost as if he'd been expecting him.

"Hey, Rev Jeb!"

Jeb glanced up to see a flatbed truck filled with teenagers cruising down Main Street. Caleb Armstrong was at the wheel, and Faith was sitting close to him while another boy occupied the passenger seat. In the back of the truck were four other teens—friends of Caleb's who all waved at Jeb.

"Dad says we can use this to build our float for the Fourth of July parade," one girl shouted.

"Looking good," Jeb shouted back. Caleb gunned the engine and tooted the horn as the truck headed on down the street. "We're going over to Eagle River for decorations," the girl shouted.

Jeb waved and headed back up the street toward the parsonage. For the first time since meeting her, he truly hoped he would not run into Megan along the way.

But Singing Springs was a small town and someone like Owen Osbourne couldn't show up after nearly ten years without someone commenting on his reappearance to someone else who then speculated on his return with a third party. So when Megan came down the stairs after changing beds and cleaning rooms and saw Reba glance at her and then focus all of her attention on the computer screen where she kept track of reservations, she suspected something was up.

"What?" she asked, well aware that one of the letters she'd picked up from the post office that morning had featured the familiar fat, loopy scrawl of Reba's daughter.

"Owen's back." Reba swiveled her chair around to face Megan. "Nellie called. She saw him walking up to the parsonage. I was hoping to have more information before we talked about how you want to handle… things."

So she hadn't imagined it. She had seen her father going into the shop. She didn't know what to think about his return.

"Fred told Nellie that Jeb invited him. Seems they met at the barbershop earlier this morning," Reba said.

Why would Jeb invite her father to the parsonage and not tell her first? Why wouldn't he have called? What if Faith ran into Owen? "I'll be back," she said and headed out the front door and up the hill to the parsonage.

With every step her fury increased—at her father, at Jeb, at whatever cruel fate had brought him back when everything was going so well. By the time she reached the house, she was breathing hard, not from exertion, but from the tightness in her chest that felt as if her heart were hardening into granite.

The two men were sitting on the porch as she came around the side of the house. The low rumble of their voices told her that neither of them was aware of her presence. When she heard her father's voice, thick with emotion and raspy with regret, her resolve faltered. Suddenly she had no idea what she would say, what she would demand, how she would achieve the one thing she'd come to accomplish—getting her father to leave before Faith knew he was back. Of course, that was an impossible task. After all, Singing Springs was a small town.

She heard the clink of a spoon against a ceramic mug and looked up to see her father sitting with his back to her in one of the four rocking chairs that lined the porch. Jeb had pulled a second rocker close to the first and was sitting forward with his forearms resting on his knees, listening intently to Owen's story.

And a story it was, Megan reminded herself. The man was a master at rewriting history.

"Hello, Owen," she said quietly as she climbed the steps to the porch. She did not look at him or Jeb, but focused on her feet, as if at any moment she might make a misstep and fall. She heard the scrape of chairs as both men stood and she still did not look up.

"You used to call me Dad," Owen replied.

"That was a long time ago." The effort to keep her voice steady and neutral almost overwhelmed her. She again swallowed the questions and accusations and fury that she'd gulped back for years.

"I'll get another mug," Jeb said and started for the door.

"Stay," Megan said, as if coaching a puppy. She pulled a third rocker into the circle and sat down. "We might as well settle this right now." She looked directly at her father for the first time.

He had aged, looking at least a decade older than his sixty years.

"Where have you been, Owen? Last I knew you'd checked yourself into the VA hospital in Milwaukee. When I came to see you they said you'd left with no forwarding address. That was nine years ago."

"I bounced around—ended up in California for a while. But I've been back at the VA for the last year." He met her gaze. "I'm sober, Megan. It's been almost four years since I had a drink."

For Owen four years was a lifetime, but Megan fought against being too impressed. "You've been at the VA all that time?" she asked, assuming he'd checked himself into some sort of program offered there. "I mean, it's one thing to stay sober living a normal life out in the world, and quite another to stay sober under the watchful eye of…"

Jeb placed his hand on her arm. "Let him tell it, Megan," he advised.

Megan slumped against the back of the rocker, folded her arms tightly across her body and pushed the chair into motion with one foot. "I'm listening."

Owen glanced over at Jeb, who nodded encouragingly. "They gave me a job—part-time, but it paid enough to keep me housed and fed." Then he sucked in a deep breath and slowly let it out. "I came back for one selfish reason, Meggie. I'm dying and I don't want to die alone."

Oh, please. Megan could not count the number of times her father had used this ruse. Well, not dying, but the remorse and the desire to be close to family and friends. It would last a month or so and then—boom— right back to his old ways. She tightened her grip on herself and said nothing.

"The docs have done what they can, but the fact is my liver is shot and I've no one to blame but myself."

Megan studied the man sitting not two feet from her and noticed for the first time the slight yellowing of his eyes and skin. Her heart thudded against her chest, warring between camps of pent-up anger and the innate compassion that had made her stay with him all those years, until Reba and Stan had taken her in and Owen had left town.

"Can't they... Isn't there medicine or a transplant? What about a transplant?" At the same time the words tumbled from her lips, she was sending up a silent prayer that rocked her to her core. *Save him, please.*

Owen smiled and shook his head. "I'm on the list, but it's a long shot." He shook off the thought and leaned toward her. "So I'm here to ask you to forgive me and let me just be here in Singing Springs. I won't bother you—or Faith. I promise. I just want to be close."

Megan closed her eyes. So many times it had happened in much the same way. Owen would go off on a bender and return days later full of apologies and compromises and promises. Bargaining with her for her forgiveness. She'd been a child—eight or nine at her earliest recollection—alone in the rundown house they shared, scared and yet covering for him when people like Nellie Barnsworth or Reverend Dunhill stopped by or called. And always, always terrified that he might not come back.

Early on she built her resources. She would drop by the house of a friend at suppertime and, of course, was invited to stay. She would suggest what fun it would be to have a sleepover, knowing her friends would never come to her house, but would invite her to theirs instead. She would appear at the inn and quietly start helping Stan weed the kitchen garden or Reba hang the laundry. And Reba would send her home with a shopping bag full of food when Megan refused to stay the night, arguing that her father would be home soon.

"Megan?" Jeb's voice was close and filled with concern.

She opened her eyes and focused on her father. "Can you work?" she asked.

"Some."

Jeb cleared his throat. "Actually, the church council has been talking about hiring a part-time person to take care of the maintenance and cleaning and such. Now that the summer folks are here and we're running the youth center every night, there's more to do."

As if the job part of the problem were solved Megan pressed on. "And where will you stay?"

Hope fired in her father's pale blue eyes. "Mike Caspin has a house trailer on his property. I'm staying there for the time being."

Mike had been her father's dearest friend. They had served together in Vietnam and he'd stood by him through everything. Mike was the one who'd often brought Owen home, helped him get cleaned up, helped him get work every time he lost a job. It did not surprise Megan that the first person Owen had sought out was not her, but Mike.

When she didn't say anything for several moments, Owen got nervous. "Hey, you can call the docs yourself," he said. "Check the story out. They'll tell you. I came to them stone-cold sober—you'll have to take my word that it had been almost four years by then. I haven't touched..."

"Why California?" She saw the quick exchange of looks between Jeb and Owen. Again Jeb nodded, clearly blessing whatever might come next. Megan leaned forward. "You went to see her?"

Owen closed his eyes, suddenly the picture of exhaustion. "There's a part of the program—AA—where you need to face what you've done and the people you've done it to. I'm working on that, but it's hard. For years I used your mother as rationalization for my drinking, and that took a toll on you and Faith. Poor me." He opened his eyes and peered at Megan. "I had choices, Meggie. It wasn't all on her."

"So did she," Megan muttered, startled by the depths of her bitterness after all these years. "She could have stayed and worked things out."

Owen shrugged. "Coulda, shoulda, woulda. It's the past and we all have our regrets about the road not taken. I expect that you do, as well," he reminded her, sounding like a parent for the first time since she'd stepped onto the porch.

"Leave Faith out of this," she snapped.

"I can't, because what your mother and I realized was that somehow through God's grace our only child had found a courage neither of us ever had. I have to tell you, Meggie, that there was a time when I couldn't stand that you were so strong and brave and determined to care for that child no matter what, when your parents had been total flops."

"And now?"

"Now, if you'll permit me, I just want the comfort of being near you and Faith for whatever time I have. I've been talking with the pastor here and, if you like, neither you nor Faith ever has to see me without him being there."

"I need to talk to Faith, see what she wants—and doesn't want."

"That's only right," Owen agreed.

She rocked for several long minutes as she processed

this stunning turn of events, then added, "And if you so much as look at a drink…"

"Agreed," he said, and something about the way he met her gaze gave her the hope that this time things would be different.

After another long and increasingly uncomfortable silence, Jeb cleared his throat. "Owen, you'll need to meet with the council about the job," Jeb said. "Do you want me to set that up?"

Owen nodded. "I'd appreciate that. Thank you."

Megan stood up and so did both men. "I'll talk to Faith tonight," Megan said. She felt her father's gaze on her, but turned away. Just before starting back down the porch steps, she asked the one thing that had haunted her for all of her life. "So why did she leave us?"

"She didn't leave us, Meggie. She left me."

"Funny. It sure feels like she left me, too," Megan said, and walked away before Jeb or her father could witness her heart breaking one more time over a woman she'd barely known.

Jeb gave Owen a ride out to Mike Caspin's farm. The house trailer was positioned close to the road, and Owen assured him that he'd either hitch into town or Mike would give him a ride if he passed the council's interview and was hired on at the church. They exchanged phone numbers, Owen giving him Mike's since he didn't have a phone in the trailer.

"Pastor, do you think I'm being selfish wanting to be close to Meggie after all this time?"

"A little," Jeb answered. The man deserved honesty. "But this isn't all about you, Owen. Megan has spent her life living for others—you and then Faith. She's kept a lot of things under wraps all these years and maybe your coming back will help her work through her past so she can move forward and make a life for herself. Just don't hurt her again," he warned.

"No, I wouldn't do that."

"Yeah, you would," Jeb told him and saw the man bristle with surprise.

"Not intentionally," Owen argued as he stood a little taller, clearly prepared for a fight.

Jeb shrugged. "No one said it was ever intentional, Owen. But hurt is hurt and all I'm saying is that, between you and her mother and Faith's father, Megan has had her full serving and then some."

"I can do this right," Owen assured him, although it sounded more like he was trying to reassure himself.

"I'll set up the interview and get back to you," Jeb said. "In the meantime, how about coming to services this Sunday with Mike and his family?"

He saw that Owen recognized the test Jeb was giving him. "I'll be there," he said.

Jeb smiled at the older man and drove away. But as he navigated the turns of the road back into town, he began to have doubts. "I'm flying blind here, God," he prayed aloud as he drove. "It feels right, but maybe I got so caught up in Owen's story. Maybe I saw a man seeking redemption—a man like I was after the accident. Did I want to save Owen because I know how it feels to be so totally lost, blaming yourself and drowning in regret?"

He swerved to miss a squirrel that darted across the road and suddenly had the thought that maybe this was what it had been like that night. Deborah had swerved, lost control and in seconds the car had been upside down in a ditch, its front crushed in and the lifeless bodies of his wife and daughter trapped inside.

"I told Owen that this wasn't all about him, but maybe what I've failed to see is that I'm tempted to make his situation all about mine. He has this last chance to make amends, to find forgiveness in the hearts of his only child and grandchild. He has this chance that I never had. Is that it, God? Am I wanting Owen to succeed because I failed so miserably?"

A horn honked impatiently behind him and he realized he'd slowed to a crawl. Shaken, he pulled to the side of the road to allow the other car to pass. And then he noticed that his hands were trembling and his breath was heaving as if he'd just run a marathon. He rested his forehead against the steering wheel. "Guide my steps as I try to help these good people," he prayed.

Another car horn sounded and he looked up. Megan had stopped her car next to his. "You okay?"

"Yeah." Jeb got out of his car and leaned one hand against her vehicle. Of all the faces Jeb might have hoped to see at that moment, Megan's was far and away the first he would have prayed to see and the last he could have imagined. And yet it was in her face that he found his answer. There were no signs that the meeting with her father had taken its toll. "What are you doing out here?" he asked.

She shrugged. "He doesn't have a car and I'm not sure how he's getting around, but he needs food and Reba had some of Stan's clothes she's been meaning to give away and he's going to need to look sharp for the council interview and…"

You love him, Jeb realized. *In spite of everything he's put you through.*

"Were you planning to stay and talk awhile with him?"

"Nope. No more talk until I have a chance to discuss this with Faith. Just drop these off and head back. We have a meeting tonight about the parade, remember? And I still have to get supper and… Why didn't you tell me he was back?"

Jeb studied her features, expecting repressed anger, and found only hurt. "I should have," he admitted. "I wanted to make sure that he'd come back for the right reasons—I mean, that he wouldn't cause you or Faith more pain."

"You wanted to protect us? How?"

"I'm not sure," Jeb admitted. "In the barbershop it seemed to me like all I was offering was a place where he could come and talk to someone trained to listen."

"But?"

"But once he showed up at the house, I don't know. I had to really fight to get a handle on my emotions, to not want to tear the guy apart for all the pain he's caused you over the years."

"That doesn't sound like the kind of pastoral care you learned in divinity school."

Jeb searched her eyes and saw forgiveness there. "Sometimes I slip." He played a little drumbeat on the roof of her car with his hands. "Tell you what—how about you take those things to Owen and meet me at the burger place at the intersection? We can grab some supper and then go on to the meeting from there."

She hesitated and he knew she was wrestling with whether having a burger with him violated her promise to Faith that they would be just friends. "Hey, it's a cheeseburger," he coaxed.

"Extra pickle and mustard?"

"You got it."

She smiled. "Okay. Give me twenty minutes—thirty tops."

Jeb returned to his car.

"And Jeb? Vanilla malt, okay?"

"You want fries with that?"

Her laughter was like a soothing balm for his spirits. "Bet you never thought you'd be saying that when you ran that big-time company," she teased. "Yeah, fries, too. If I'm going to clog the arteries might as well go all the way." She waved out the open window as she drove away.

Jeb stood in the street, watching her go. She was the most remarkably resilient person he'd ever known, and he was all too aware that he was falling in love with Megan Osbourne.

Chapter Eleven

The Fourth of July dawned sunny and warm—perfect weather for a parade. Tourists and locals alike came early to reserve their places along the parade route with collapsible chairs, blankets, strollers and coolers on wheels that doubled as benches. It seemed everyone was decked out in some combination of red, white and blue and the crowd was easily triple what it had been on Memorial Day. The streets buzzed with chatter, laughter and anticipation that was almost palpable.

But Megan had too much on her mind and frankly the crowds, the traffic and the general confusion were more irritating than inspiring. To her surprise the church council had unanimously approved hiring Owen as the custodian. True, they had made it clear the hiring was probationary—in this case, one strike and out. But these were people who had known Owen for decades—knew his history, knew how many times he'd made promises he couldn't keep. Were they setting him up to fail?

No, they wouldn't do that, she thought. On the contrary, it seemed as if several people were working hard to make sure that Owen didn't fail. Reba had invited him for supper—along with Jeb—two or three times a week since his return to Singing Springs. And Megan had to admit that those occasions had gone far better than she might have imagined. Faith seemed to be fascinated with her grandfather, encouraging him to tell stories of hopping an empty boxcar to save money on his way to California, and to describe the scenery, the weather, the people there and how it differed from Wisconsin.

Just the night before, while she and Jeb were washing the dishes, Owen and Faith had disappeared and when she went looking for them, she'd found them sitting together on the inn's porch swing. Owen had his arm around Faith's shoulders and was talking to her in low tones.

"What was that about?" Megan had asked her father later, after Faith had gone to bed.

"She's worried that boy she's running with will dump her when summer's over," Owen said.

"And what did you tell her?" Megan fought against the wave of jealousy she felt that Faith would have such a conversation with this man she hardly knew, rather than with her own mother.

"I told her she was probably reading things right. I told her, knowing that, it would be important for her to watch herself. I told her there probably was no more she could do to make that boy stay with her than…"

He hesitated and Megan froze.

"Tell me you didn't say something about my not being able to make Danny stay so she'd have a father."

Owen bristled. "What I said was 'no more than I could make your grandmother stay once she made up her mind to go.' I have no idea what you might have done to make that Moreland boy stay. I'm sure you remember that I was too drunk most of the time to care." He got up and stalked off down the road.

Megan had thought of going after him the way she had dozens of times when she was a girl, but her feet felt rooted to the floorboards of the porch. She couldn't believe he had changed so much that going after him would make any more difference this time than it had back then.

Jeb had come out on the porch then. The way he'd rested his hands on her shoulders as she watched her father disappear around a corner told her that he'd heard most of her conversation with Owen.

"If he's going to drink, nothing I can do will stop him—short of praying," she'd said without waiting for Jeb's comment.

"There's one more thing," Jeb had said, resting his cheek against her hair. "You can love him in spite of his flaws."

"I do," she'd protested, and knew it for the lie that it was the minute the words were airborne. "It's complicated."

"He wants to make it this time, Megan. He's put his past to rest, taken responsibility for the damage done and finally come to understand that he has something to live for—you and Faith."

"Too bad he didn't come to this epiphany until he found out he was dying." She hated the bile of bitterness that filled her thoughts and words.

"We're all dying, Megan. It comes with the package. The trick is to live and love fully every hour and day without the assurance of more time. Owen may have come to that realization late in life, but it's not too late. Not for him. Not if you'll meet him halfway."

And later when she was in bed and staring out at the black night, Megan thought of her father stumbling

along the narrow road that led from the tavern or convenience store back to Mike's farm. She envisioned him
alone inside the small trailer, slumped onto the sofa that
doubled as his bed. The images were vivid because she
did not have to use her imagination—only her memory.
Her eyes filled with tears that leaked down her temples
and into her hair. Her chest heaved with sobs as she
prayed that this time—please, God—was different.

But with the dawning of Independence Day Megan
awoke with a sense of dread. The holidays had always
triggered the worst binges. And so she'd been up before
dawn, driven out to the trailer, banged on the door and
found it unlocked. Inside everything was pristine—no
dishes in the sink, no sign of beer or other spirits, no sign
that her father had been there at all. Her heart quickened
with panic and she drove slowly back into town,
checking the ditches and fields along the way for any
sign of him.

By the time she got back to the inn, the parade was
beginning to assemble up the hill in the church parking
lot. *Jeb,* she thought as she hurried up the hill. He would
know what to do.

She reached the parking lot, breathless with worry and
exertion. "Faith," she called, "have you seen Rev Jeb?"

Faith motioned toward the church, then turned her attention back to Caleb and his friends as they finished
adding bunting to the youth center's float.

Megan thought of the advice her father had offered
Faith. Good advice and just maybe, coming from him, she
would take it. Megan hurried into the church vestibule.
It was ten degrees cooler in there and she paused for a
moment to catch her breath before heading toward the
sound of voices floating up from the basement.

And then she heard familiar laughter. Not Jeb's, but her father's. The sound tugged at her memories of better times, times when he had held her on his knee, times before her mother had left them both, long ago and nearly forgotten times when they had been a family.

She pulled open the heavy carved door leading to the sanctuary. "Dad," she cried, her voice echoing with relief in the empty church.

Owen startled and turned toward the sound as if he couldn't believe what he was hearing. When Megan reached him and touched her fingers to his face, peering deeply into his eyes, he hesitated only a minute before hugging her. "You haven't called me that in years, Meggie," he murmured as she broke down sobbing against his shoulder.

"I went to the trailer and you weren't there, I thought… I'm so sorry."

"Shh, little girl. You had every reason to think that. I've got a long road ahead of me before you're going to trust me and I just hope I have the time to make it all the way."

"Don't talk like that," Megan said, pulling free of him and swiping at her tears with the backs of her hands. "Oh, my." She gulped as she really looked at him for the first time. "Look at you." She straightened the oversize red, white and blue bow tie he was wearing and then took another step back. "Look at you," she repeated and grinned. Her father was in full costume—minus the beard—to play Uncle Sam in the parade.

Owen blushed. "It was Faith's idea. That granddaughter of mine has a way of talking folks into things. I seem to recall you were that way once."

Megan couldn't seem to stop grinning. Her father was right here, stone-cold sober and wearing a costume to boot. "But where did you go last night? The trailer looks…"

"He ended up here," Jeb said. "We talked about some things and before we knew it the rooster was crowing, so your dad sacked out on the couch for a couple of hours."

"You need your rest," Megan fussed, peering closely to see just how exhausted he was.

"And I'll have it right after we get this show on the road. You watching or riding the float?"

Megan gave a little shriek. She'd forgotten all about the parade. Her costume was back at the house. "Riding the float," she said with a wave. "Wait for me."

As far as Jeb was concerned there could never have been a Pilgrim lovelier than Megan Osbourne. She wore a simple high-necked gray dress adorned with a wide, white, starched collar and apron. She was seated on the front of the float that the kids had decorated to resemble a boat landing at a huge rock. When Jessica had suggested that Jeb play the part of the Pilgrim man, Megan had been quick to suggest that Rick Epstein would be good for that role. "Jeb would make a wonderful Thomas Jefferson."

The float was designed to show three key episodes in the founding of the country—the Pilgrims' landing at Plymouth Rock, Thomas Jefferson writing the Declaration of Independence and finally Owen as Uncle Sam holding the American flag. Understanding that Megan was concerned that they not be portrayed as a couple, even in storybook fashion, Jeb had seconded the idea of playing Jefferson. But after the parade, he had every intention of spending the better part of this day with Megan—and to his relief, Reba had agreed to help.

"Ladies and gentlemen, gather round for the annual silent Cakewalk auction," Pete Burbank shouted through the handheld bullhorn later that afternoon when everyone had gathered in the park. "Here's how this works. Gentlemen, line up here and when I call your name pick one cake. The maker of that cake is your dinner partner this evening, so choose carefully. And please don't drop the cakes, gents. Those delectable creations are our dessert for the evening."

Everyone chuckled at that and also because most people knew that at least the married men were well aware which cake belonged to their wives. Thanks to Reba, Jeb had the inside track on which cake Megan had contributed.

"Rev Jeb, why don't you get things started?"

Jeb took his time studying each cake. He could see Megan standing on the fringe of the crowd, pressed against the roped-off barricade, but he didn't let on that he knew she was there. He started to pick up one cake, heard a gasp from Nellie Barnsworth, and then set it back down. He deliberately passed by Megan's cake and saw her brow furrow in what he hoped was disappointment. He was hoping that in spite of her reservations, there was no one she'd rather spend the evening with than him. After all, who could question their being together when the cause was a blind test like the cakewalk?

"Rev Jeb?" Pete spoke into the bullhorn. "You take much more time and it's gonna be dark," he chided. The crowd laughed.

Jeb grinned and started back up the row of cakes, again passing Megan's with barely a glance. "I'll take…" He waved his hand over three cakes, none of them Megan's, and then turned suddenly and picked hers up. "This one."

Reba let out a whoop and everyone applauded as he handed the cake to Jessica for the women to slice for the picnic, and Pete called out Megan's name.

"Ms. Osbourne," Jeb said with a bow, and then as he joined her to watch the rest of the contest, muttered, "Had you worried, did I?"

"Don't flatter yourself," she whispered, but she was smiling and her fingers tightened on his arm.

Later, after they filled their plates with barbecued chicken, homemade coleslaw, potato salad and corn on the cob, Jeb led the way to a shaded area overlooking the lake. Megan followed, carrying cups filled with lemonade.

"I didn't have a chance to really thank you for taking my father in last night," she said as she sat down on the blanket he'd spread for them.

"He's a good man at heart, Megan."

"I was so afraid that…"

Jeb covered her hand with his. "I know, but he wants to make it this time, Megan—for you and Faith. He doesn't want your last memories of him to be…what they would have been had he not come back. He told me a lot of things last night and I have to say that, in your shoes, it would be hard for me to forgive some of it."

"Oh, Jeb, I've forgiven him, but he's always been a weak man—someone who tried but failed at so many of the important things in life. You can't blame me for worrying about how he might disappoint Faith. I mean, you've seen how she's taken to him."

"Like a father?" He waited while realization dawned.

"Exactly," she murmured.

Jeb took a bite of his chicken and chewed it slowly, buying time, wondering if he would overstep his bounds to suggest what he'd been thinking. His role as her pastor and spiritual advisor kept getting in the way of his feelings for her. *May the words of my mouth...* The ancient prayer was one he had relied on often—one that had never failed him in the past. "Megan?"

She looked up at him.

"Have you ever thought about contacting Faith's father—about putting them in touch with each other?"

The anguish that spread across every feature of her face gave him his answer. "Oh, Jeb, you can't imagine how I've agonized over that. I mean, I didn't intentionally keep them apart, but what if Danny rejects her? What if he's still in denial about even being her father? And even if he isn't, wouldn't I just be ripping open the wound she's carried all her life, knowing he didn't want her?"

"Have you talked about this at all with Jessica?"

"Yeah. Jess thinks that Danny stays away because he knows Faith is his, knows he left us both to face the gossip and speculation, and can't face his own guilt. She thinks that's why he always arranges these elaborate holiday family gatherings in places like Disneyland or Vail or Mexico. When their parents died, they were living in Milwaukee so he didn't even have to come here for the funerals."

"But she doesn't know for sure that he's feeling guilt or remorse?"

"No. She admits that she hasn't brought it up. She just thinks the evidence is there—two failed marriages, and having to accept that success and money aren't the true path to happiness that he always believed they would be."

"And Faith? What does she think?"

"We haven't talked about it in a long time. She's been so happy and doing so well with the way things are. I mean, life with Reba and me seems perfectly normal to her. She has other friends who live with their mothers and rarely see their fathers. She doesn't seem to think about him much at all anymore."

"Megan, think about her recent actions—the way she spends all her time with Caleb, her concern that you and I might start seeing each other romantically, and now turning to her grandfather instead of you or Reba for advice."

"There's no connection," Megan said, but she was biting her lower lip the way he'd learned she did when she was worried.

"There is a connection. We're all male and perhaps subconsciously we represent to Faith the various sides of that father she never knew."

"I don't know what you mean."

"I'm no shrink, but perhaps her relationship with Caleb is a kind of fantasy of the way her father might have loved her, might have taken pride and joy in her the way Caleb sometimes does. But at the same time she's wise enough to understand that the likely outcome of this is that he'll leave at the end of the summer and that will be it for any romance between them. So Caleb doesn't quite fit the bill."

"So who are you then?"

He shrugged. "Maybe I'm the threat, the man who could potentially take you away from her. And then Owen shows up—someone she can feel safe casting in the role of father. But what happens when Owen gets sicker? What happens if he dies before he can get a transplant? She's right back where she started."

"And what if Dan rejects her—or worse, what if he…she…" Megan bit her lip hard and turned away.

"Say it out loud, Megan. What is it that you fear most?"

"It's selfish," she warned. "So shamefully selfish."

"Say it anyway."

"I'm afraid she'll want to be with him and not me. He can give her so much and take her so many places and make the road ahead smoother for her without having to worry about scholarships or working to help with the tuition or… Why are you pushing this?" she asked, her eyes suddenly furious.

"Because I'm also selfish—I don't think there can be a future for you and me unless you first resolve all of those past relationships that hurt you so much. And yet those relationships helped mold you into the strong and beautiful person you've become." He cupped her cheek in his palm. "I'm falling in love with you, Megan, and I find myself dreaming of a future that includes you and Faith and, with God's blessing, children of our own."

Jeb had thought he was prepared for any reaction but the one he got. Megan scrambled to her feet and hastily gathered her picnic dishes, not looking at him. He could see that her hands were shaking and he stood up as well, reaching for her shoulder, but she shrugged him off. "I have to go," she mumbled, and took off across the park, holding her long Pilgrim skirt with one hand.

Chapter Twelve

Megan's heart and her head seemed ready to explode. There were so many things that had come all at once. Her father's return, Jeb's suggestion that maybe it was time Faith knew her own father, and then on top of everything he was talking about the two of them marrying and having children. It was too much.

The very idea that she and Jeb might marry was surely ludicrous. He was infatuated with her—that was it. She had surprised him on a number of levels and he was intrigued by that. How could a minister possibly consider her a proper wife? Somehow she had to make him see that in many ways what they had discovered in each other was only a more mature version of what Faith and Caleb shared. It couldn't last in either case.

"And I'd like to know why not," Reba demanded, after she had witnessed Megan's flight and followed her back to the inn.

"Let me count the ways," Megan moaned.

"You cannot let stereotypical ideals of what a

preacher's wife looks like shape your thinking on this, Meggie. You can't let people like Nellie or her ilk influence your decision."

"I'm not," Megan protested, but deep down she knew she was. The town matriarch and her cohorts had long held sway over how she viewed herself. She had spent years trying to prove herself to them, trying to make sure that Faith was not punished or discriminated against simply by virtue of her birth. And she had succeeded to a point, but she couldn't see them embracing the idea of Jeb marrying her. They would turn on Jeb and that would be a disaster for the community. "Besides, I have to think of what's best for Faith."

"Seems to me giving that girl a real home with two loving parents and the possibility of siblings wouldn't be a bad thing." Reba had softened her tone and she was sitting close to Megan on the inn's porch swing, her hand resting lightly on Megan's knee.

"And this idea of bringing Dan into the picture…" Megan released a deep shuddering sigh.

"Now, that's another matter altogether. It might just be the right thing to do, especially now with Faith seeing Owen and you and thinking on that. However, the way I see it, Faith can make that decision herself. You can give her all the information she needs and your blessing if she wants to make contact, and leave it in God's hands from there."

Megan took some time to consider this. Faith was mature for her age and it certainly was her right to know her real father. "What if he rejects her, denies ever fathering her?"

"Times have changed. Folks do DNA tests at the drop of a hat these days. You can prove he's the father—

you could have proved it then, but he left and you were dead set against going after him."

"Oh, Reba, it would never have worked. He would have resented me and eventually Faith for the life he'd missed out on."

Reba snorted. "Well, this is no longer all about Mr. Danny Moreland—never was, truth be told. You're sometimes so wrapped up in making sure everybody else is okay that you forget to take care of what you want and need. Always trying to please others. Why don't you try pleasing yourself for once?"

Megan looked over at the woman who was as much a mother to her as any woman could have been. Reba's face was flushed and she worked her mouth the way she did when something upset her. "Why are you so mad at me?" she asked, and to her astonishment Reba burst into tears.

"Oh, Meggie, I was hoping not to have to tell you this until later. You and Jeb were having such a good time today, and I just wanted this day for the two of you to share and enjoy and…"

"Reba, what's happened? Are you sick?"

"No more than usual," Reba said as she reached in the pocket of her apron and pulled out one of Stan's old handkerchiefs. She gave a snort of a laugh as she blew her nose. "Seems you and me both need to face facts, Meggie."

Megan felt her heart clutch. *No, please, no more,* she prayed silently. She really didn't think she could face anything else today. "Tell me." She folded her hands tightly in her lap, steeling herself for what was coming.

"This is probably the last season for the inn—at least for my running the inn," Reba said. "I just can't do it anymore, honey. The pain from my arthritis too often gets in the way of how I treat guests. In town the other day I overheard that young honeymoon couple talking about the inn and they said…" The tears started again and Megan grabbed Reba's hand and held on. "They said the inn was fabulous, with the one exception of the crab behind the desk."

"That's just cruel," Megan said. "And it's one opinion. Surely…"

"They didn't know I heard them, honey, and it's not just one opinion. I've seen it in the way other guests react—like they're not sure how to approach me if they need something."

"But…"

"Besides, you and I have known this day would come. You've seen the letters and e-mails from my Carla down in Arizona. She worries and she's got a husband and three kids to manage, not to mention a job. I'd be easing her burden some by going down there, but I laid down the law on one thing. I'll spend my summers right here—keep the house and sell the inn."

Megan tried to imagine the inn without Reba and couldn't.

"So you see, here's one more reason for you to think seriously about what Jeb said to you about a future with him. I don't want to have to sit down there in the desert worrying about you, missy."

"Faith…"

"Faith will be fine. You, on the other hand, have come to a fork in the road. The way I see it, you can take the high road up the hill to living in that parsonage with the man who has come to love you like you deserve to be loved. Or you can insist on continuing to decide what you think everybody else needs and ignoring yourself. What's it going to be?"

"It's not that simple."

"Sure it is, honey. But there's time yet. I'm not going anywhere until the fall. In the meantime, Pete Burbank might be interested in buying the inn and I already told him that, whoever ends up buying it, you have a job and a home here for as long as you want. I'm not selling on any other terms," Reba declared in a voice she might have used to deliver an ultimatum from the church pulpit.

The older woman shifted her weight and pushed herself off the swing, groaning with every movement. "Got to stir around a bit," she said. "You stay on here if you like. All the guests are still out for the evening. Beautiful night for sitting on a porch swing and thinking things through."

"Reba?" Megan looked up at her friend and mentor. "I love you."

"I know, honey. I know. Now, take my advice and turn some of that boundless love you offer others inside and love yourself for a change." She lumbered into the lobby of the inn, letting the screen door close softly behind her.

Megan pushed the swing into motion and kept the rhythm going until she saw the first of the fireworks light the night sky over the lake. It was unlike her to wish time away, but she couldn't help wondering where she would be and what her life would be like a year from now.

"Hey, Mom."

Megan was surprised to see Faith standing at the foot of the porch steps.

"Hey, yourself." Megan patted the seat next to her. "Want to watch the fireworks with me?"

Faith scrambled up to the porch and curled herself onto the swing, one leg tucked under her. "Reba coming?"

Watching the fireworks together on the Fourth had been one of their longstanding traditions. It was during a fireworks display that Reba and Stan had suggested Megan bring Faith and come live with them. It had always been a special time for them—a family time.

"Where's Caleb?"

Faith shrugged. "His older brother has some of his fraternity friends staying over and Caleb wanted to be with them."

"He didn't ask you to come?"

"He asked. I turned him down."

Megan rested her arm along the back of the swing. "Oh, honey, that's so sweet, but…"

"They'll be drinking, Mom."

"Oh."

Faith squirmed around until she had fit herself in the shelter of Megan's arm, resting her head on her mother's shoulder the way she had as a child. "I don't like Caleb's brother. I mean, he seems like a nice guy, really outgoing, and all the girls think he's even better-looking than Caleb. But he's not nearly as nice as Caleb."

"I see." It was times like this that Megan sent up a prayer that God would guide her words. "How is he not so nice?"

"For one thing, if it's not all about him, he gets upset, puts people down, especially Caleb. And sometimes the way he looks at me like he's trying to size me up or something." She shivered. "And he's always talking about drinking parties they throw in the frat house."

"Well, then you were wise to stay away. I'm sure Caleb will understand."

"Yeah. Probably." She didn't sound very sure of that.

Megan wrapped her arms around her daughter and

rested her chin on Faith's silky hair as they watched the fireworks together. *Thank you, God, for this wonderful child.*

"So where's Rev Jeb?" Faith asked, just when Megan was beginning to feel that the silence between them was comfortable.

"Not sure. I guess I kind of dumped him."

Faith sat up and peered at Megan's face. "For real?"

"Would that make you happy?"

She watched as her daughter wrestled with an answer. "No, because I know you'd be sad. He's not so bad. Gramps says that he's a keeper. Auntie Reba thinks the man walks on water and Gramps says that if Jeb makes you happy, what's my problem."

Megan had noticed that Faith quoted her grandfather with growing frequency. "And what do you say?"

"He's okay. I just don't want— I just worry about…"

"Hey, you and I are both savvy women, honey. I can see the pros and cons of being with Jeb the same way I know you realize the ups and downs of seeing Caleb."

"Except I know there's no future for Caleb and me— not really. Not like there could be for you and Rev Jeb."

"You think so?"

"Mom, the way the man looks at you has the female population of Singing Springs drooling with envy. And then that business today with the cakewalk—like he didn't know which cake was yours." Faith settled back into the curve of Megan's arm as a spray of gold lit the night sky. "I mean, how romantic can you get?"

Megan smiled, realizing that Faith wasn't offering her permission to continue seeing Jeb. She was giving it her blessing. She hugged the girl close. "I love you, Faith Osbourne."

"Love you back," Faith replied and then sat up and hugged her knees to her. "Here comes the grand finale," she shrieked as a series of red, blue and gold fireworks streaked their way heavenward.

Megan watched until the last ember had burned itself out, the last pop and boom had echoed across the lake. And in the silence that followed she knew that Reba was right. It was time she stopped living to make up for yesterday and started looking toward tomorrow.

"You coming up to the house?" Faith asked as she stood and stretched and yawned.

"In a bit. You go ahead and check on Reba to be sure she took her medicine, okay?"

Faith saluted and yawned again. "I am beat." She leaned down and kissed Megan's cheek. "See you in the morning, okay?"

"Sleep well."

After Faith left, Megan sat for a while longer, watching the crowd disperse. She saw Jeb walking across the road and up the lane to the parsonage. He called out good-nights to several locals and continued on his way alone.

Jeb could not have been more surprised when Megan fell into step next to him. "Hi," she said, her voice husky with the damp night air.

"Hi, yourself," he replied, taking care not to read too much into her sudden appearance. "Did you see the fireworks?"

"Faith and I watched from the porch at the inn. Kind of a family tradition."

"Sounds nice."

"You got a few minutes? I'd like to talk."

Was she asking to speak with her pastor or with the man who loved her? "Sure. I could make us some coffee."

"That would be nice."

They walked the rest of the short distance to the parsonage in silence. Inside, Jeb flicked on lights and started preparing the coffee. "I'm not much of a cook," he said, making small talk until he could get a read on her purpose in coming here. "But I make one terrific cup of joe."

Megan smiled and wandered into the living room where he'd left a lamp on and the windows open to catch a cross breeze. She fingered the lace curtains. "I always loved these curtains," she said. "Mrs. Dunhill brought them back from a trip she and the reverend took to Ireland."

The coffee dripping into the pot filled the silence.

"I expect you had a chance to travel some when you were in business," she added.

"Some." *Where was this going?*

The coffeemaker gave a final shudder and spit out the last of the brew. Jeb got mugs and spoons and a small pitcher of milk. "I'm out of cream," he called.

"Milk's fine."

He set things up on the kitchen table. "Come and get it," he said.

She returned to the kitchen and poured milk into her mug and then the hot coffee. He filled his mug with black coffee and pulled out a chair for her.

"Could we sit in there?" she asked, nodding back toward the shadowy living room.

"Sure." Jeb's heart plummeted. She was deliberately choosing a venue where it would be difficult to see her face. He envisioned her in the upholstered straight chair on one side of the fireplace, with him sitting opposite her in Dunhill's worn leather recliner.

To his surprise she curled into a corner of the sofa. "Come sit with me," she invited.

Okay, so this wasn't a pastoral meeting. Jeb perched on the edge of the sofa, cradling his coffee mug with both hands. His heart was hammering so hard against his chest that he thought she must be able to hear it. But she showed no sign that she did—just took a sip of coffee and watched the gentle lift and fall of the lace curtains at the open window behind them.

"About before," Jeb began, unable to restrain himself any longer.

"Jeb, I'm sorry for running away like that. It's been a day filled with surprises." She told him about Reba's decision to sell the inn and live in Arizona half the year.

"The town won't be the same without her," he said.

"Well, she has to do what's best for her situation." Another sip of coffee and then she set the mug down on the glass-topped coffee table. "As do I."

"You mean for you and Faith?"

"No. Faith's immediate future is pretty well set. I talked to Reba about your idea of her reconnecting with her father, and Reba suggested that I give her the information she needs to do that if she chooses and leave it at that. What do you think?"

"Makes sense. She's close to Jessica and that could be a link of sorts, if she wants it."

"That's what I thought. And regardless of how she chooses to use that information, she's heading into her senior year and then college. It's a magical time in her life—in any girl's life," she added wistfully.

Except for yours, Jeb thought.

"And while life doesn't come with guarantees, she's going to have that time with all of its joys and challenges."

"You've given her that gift, Megan."

She smiled. "I guess in some ways, yes. And then there's Owen—Dad. This morning when I thought I would find him passed out in the trailer and then he wasn't there, even thinking the worst of him I was so afraid. I prayed so hard as I searched every roadside ditch and field. And then there he was—safe and sober. Do you know how many times I wished for that when I was younger? That it would be different?"

"Maybe this time it is."

"If he can just hang on," she murmured, "maybe this time…"

"I still have some contacts in the medical field in Chicago, Megan. If you and Owen agree, I could make some calls, see if there are any new treatments available."

Her smile was like sunshine coming from behind a cloud. She reached across the distance between them and grabbed his hand. "Would you? Oh, Jeb, that would be so wonderful. Even if there's nothing, at least we would know for sure that we're doing everything we can."

"I'll make some calls first thing Monday." He set his coffee down and took her hand in his, shifting his body so that they were sitting side by side on the sofa.

"So that leaves us," she said, toying with his fingers by lacing hers between each of his.

Chapter Thirteen

Jeb searched for the exact right way to phrase his next question. After all, a few hours earlier Megan had run away when he'd started talking about a future for the two of them. "Okay, let's talk about us. You first."

It was a royal cop-out and he knew it, but he also needed more information if he wasn't going to mess this up again.

"Well, it seems like everyone around me is making plans for the future, and most of them are telling me it's past time that I did the same."

"So, where do I fit in?" He took a risk and put his arm around her shoulders. She did not pull away.

"I'm not sure. I have to admit that life seemed a lot simpler when I could worry about others. I'm not comfortable thinking about myself."

Jeb couldn't help himself. "That may be the understatement of the year," he said with a chuckle.

"Yeah. I know." A smile skittered across her lips. "Out of practice."

"It's been a long time," he agreed. "Maybe I can help?"

"I don't see how. That's what I came to tell you. I need to find my way through this. Maybe then…"

"How about we find that path together?" He rested his forehead against hers. "We can start by talking through the what-ifs."

"What's that?"

"Well, for example, what if you knew for sure that Owen was going to make it this time, that Faith was going to sail through her senior year and enroll in the college of her dreams, that Reba was going to actually enjoy her life in Arizona? If you knew all of that, then what would you want for yourself? What would your life look like, Megan?"

"I don't know. I've never really stopped to think about it. Maybe go back to school?"

"Okay, say you did that. Why would you do it? I mean, is the degree something you've always wanted for yourself?"

She shrugged uncomfortably. "Not really. It just seems to matter."

"To who?"

She didn't answer so he stated the obvious. "You think it matters to others—maybe even to me. But you're wrong, Megan. The people who matter in your life will love you for who you are, not because you have some résumé of degrees and accomplishments."

"How can you say it won't matter if we— If you—"

Jeb stroked her hair. "Ah, now we're getting to the crux of things. In the business world we used to ask job candidates where they saw themselves being in their careers in five years."

"Why?"

"It was a measure of their ambition and self-confidence.

One young woman that I was interviewing to be my assistant looked me right in the eye and replied, 'Sitting where you are today.'"

It earned him a half smile. "What did you say?"

"I laughed and then I hired her on the spot."

"And where was she after five years?"

"She had left to start her own company—ever hear of ShooBags?"

"Of course. Every woman in America knows that brand. They make affordable handbags and shoes that are fun and colorful and unique. That's her?"

Jeb nodded. "I always kidded her that I had to make sure she headed down her own path so I could keep my job."

"You must have been such a good boss—leader."

"But at what cost, Megan? I put my personal life on hold and time ran out on us."

He saw that Megan was about to seize on that and turn the tables so that they were talking about him, about his path to this place. "Megan, what if you could see a future for the two of us? What would that look like?"

She heaved a sigh that completely broke the intimacy of the mood and began pacing the small cramped living room. "Be realistic, Jeb. We're not starry-eyed kids. We're well aware of how things work in the real world, and these days ministers do not take up with, much less marry, unwed mothers."

"I don't believe that." Jeb settled back on the sofa and watched her pace. "First of all, you are so much more than some label you allowed others to stamp on you, then kept on wearing like a neon sign, even after most people had long moved past the stereotype."

"That's hardly fair," she snapped. "You haven't walked in my shoes. You have no idea what it's been like."

"You could have changed that. Somewhere along the way you could have taken Faith and moved to another town, gotten a job, maybe even gone to school. But you stayed." He let that idea sink in, then added, "Sometimes inaction is in and of itself an action, Megan. You chose to stay here. No one forced you."

"Circumstances forced me. Where was I going to go? I was seventeen with a high school diploma and a baby."

"You didn't stay seventeen forever and Faith did not remain a baby. Reba gave you experience at the inn that could have translated to other markets. And still you stayed." He was pushing her and knew it, but it seemed important even though he understood it might ruin his chances of ever building a future with her.

She stood at the fireplace for a long moment, resting her fists on the cold black marble of the mantel. "Why are you doing this?"

He waited a long moment and then fully opened the door to his heart. "Because I'm in love with you."

When she didn't say anything, didn't look at him, didn't move a muscle, he wondered if he'd actually spoken aloud. He pushed himself off the sofa and went to her, resting his hands on her shoulders as he turned her to face him. In the light of the single small table lamp, he saw her eyes glisten with tears and knew she'd heard him.

"I never thought I would say those words again, Megan. I thought I could never forgive myself enough to permit myself to offer love again. But I'm offering it to you. I'm far from perfect, but if you would agree to let me try, I promise you that I will love you with every fiber of my being."

"Oh, Jeb, you deserve so much better."

"Now, there you go again putting me—and others—

on pedestals. Besides, God seems to be driving this thing. I had four other offers for my first job, knew not the first thing about Singing Springs, and ended up here. Then came the rains and the flooded basement and leaky roof, and where did I end up? Living at the inn where you and I would be together every day."

"I think that may have been more Reba's doing than God's," Megan said.

"God sometimes chooses His messenger. Let's not let life come between us, Megan. Let's walk through it together. I believe that there's a higher force at work here and we need to pay attention, unless…"

It struck him then that Megan had never really given any sign that she returned his feelings. His male pride had made him assume she cared for him as much as he had come to care for her. But what if Danny Moreland had been the true love of her life? What if she'd never married because she still loved the father of her child, in spite of his abandonment? He suddenly felt as unsure of himself as a high school freshman with a crush on the prettiest girl in class.

"Hey, if I've misread this whole thing, tell me, okay?"

She reached up and cupped his face with her palms. "I think I fell in love with you that first Sunday when I saw you in the pulpit. At least I remember thinking, why couldn't someone like you have come along years ago? Of course, then I spent the rest of the service praying for God's forgiveness for harboring such thoughts in church."

"What was it that caught your eye? My good looks? My sparkling wit? My engaging personality?"

"Your humility," she said, ruffling his hair and laughing. But then she threaded her fingers through his hair and her expression grew serious. "I do love you, Jeb, and if you think…"

"I do," he assured her, and this time he didn't have to announce his intention to kiss her. This time she met him halfway.

Jeb walked her home. They held hands like sweethearts and were suddenly shy with each other, neither saying much until they reached the back porch of Reba's small house.

"Big day," Megan said and burst into giggles.

Jeb grinned. "You could say that. Hey, if you want to wait on this, that's okay. I mean, now that I know you feel the same way…"

"No. You're right. Our love for each other harms no one. There are those who may not approve, but I've been down that road and you know what? Eventually you turn a corner and things are better."

"No more second thoughts?"

"Second, third and fifteenth," she admitted. "But we both know there are no certainties in this life. I'm here for as long as you want me."

He stepped back to look at her and frowned. Megan's heart leapt to her throat. "What?"

"I'm just trying to picture you as an old woman. You'll still be beautiful."

She slapped her hand against his chest. "You scared me," she chided. "I thought…"

Jeb caught her hands and pressed his lips to her fingers. "Here's what I know for sure, Megan. I love you and I cannot wait to get started on the life we're going to build together. We'll have our troubles and trials, but never doubt my love for you."

"I have to take things slow—for Faith's sake," she warned. "You understand that it could be a year or more before…"

He folded her into the cocoon of his arms and kissed her. "I know. Now get some sleep," he instructed. "We have that party at the center to set up tomorrow."

Megan stayed up half the night pacing her room and trying to decide how best to tell Faith—and Reba—that she and Jeb were in love. Reba would be thrilled, of course, but Faith was another matter altogether. Although she'd given her blessing for Megan and Jeb to date, had she really thought they might fall in love? Had Faith realized how life might change for al three of them?

Just before dawn she stood at her window and watched the sun fight its way through a bank of clouds turned orange, vermilion and red by the fanned rays. *Red sky in the morning,* she thought, *sailors take warning.*

While she had hoped for a quiet moment with Faith, Megan knew that was wishing for the moon and stars. Reba was up early, limping around the kitchen and fretting about the humidity and its effect on her aching joints. Then Owen stopped by.

"I could use a cup of coffee, if that's okay," he said. "I want to get up to the church and get that trim painted before the sun gets much hotter or the storms break—whichever comes first."

Megan filled a mug, set it in front of him and then did the same for Reba.

"You got in late," Reba commented, as if she were simply making idle conversation.

"I did," Megan replied and continued mixing the coffee cake she was preparing for the guests.

"Morning," Faith mumbled as she pulled out a chair and poured herself a glass of milk.

"And you're up early," Reba said. "The world is topsy-turvy."

"I'm helping Gramps with the painting and then we have to decorate the center for tonight's hoedown and…"

Megan slid the coffee cake into the oven and turned to face the three of them. "I have something to tell you. I thought I would talk to you each individually, but since you're all here and—" she glanced at the clock "—and we have a few minutes…"

"What is it, child?" Reba asked, half rising as if to test Megan's temperature with the back of her hand.

"I'm not sick," Megan assured her. "I'm in love."

"Same thing," Owen muttered.

But Megan was watching Faith, who was drawing patterns on the condensation on her juice glass as if she were facing a final exam.

"With Jeb," Megan added. "And he loves me." *Say something, Faith.*

"Oh, honey," Reba blubbered, "I'm so glad the two of you finally woke up and saw what's been right there in front of the rest of us for some time now."

"Faith?"

"Are you getting married then?" She was still working on the glass although she had already scraped it clear of any residue.

"That's a long way off, honey. We're both just getting used to the idea—as you are."

"'Cause I'd kind of like it if I could help you plan the wedding." Faith mumbled in a voice so soft that

Megan thought she must have heard wrong. Then Faith looked up at her and smiled. "Like Auntie Reba said— it's about time."

Then she was out of her chair and hugging Megan, and the two of them were dancing around the kitchen together, talking on top of each other as Faith tossed out her ideas for a spring wedding.

"Let's not get ahead of ourselves," Megan said. "Jeb hasn't asked me."

"Details," Faith and Reba said in unison, then all three women giggled.

"Just after graduation would be perfect," Faith said. "Don't you think so, Auntie Reba?"

But then all three women sobered. It was unlikely that Reba would be around to help with the planning. The inn traditionally shut down for the season the last week in October, and soon after that Reba would be on her way to Arizona.

Owen glanced up in the sudden silence. "What's wrong with September? You can more likely count on the weather." He pushed back his chair and set his empty mug in the sink. Then on his way to the back door, he awkwardly patted Megan's shoulder. "I'm happy for you, Meggie. Real happy," he said and then hurried out the door.

Megan watched him go, noticing how gaunt and frail he'd become. "Faith, would you take care of serving breakfast to the guests this morning?" Megan asked as she watched her father walk slowly up the hill toward the church. "I'll help Dad with the painting."

"Sure."

Megan grabbed a baseball cap from the rack near the door and an old paint-spattered shirt from the closet, then stopped and put her hands on Faith's shoulders.

"You're sure you're okay with this?" she asked. "I mean, with Jeb and me?"

"Mom, I've been acting like a kid—something Auntie Reba and Gramps have been only too thrilled to point out to me. I want you to be happy and if Rev Jeb makes you happy then go for it. But understand that I intend to let him know that if he hurts you, he will have to deal with me."

"And me," Reba said, taking a stand next to Faith.

"Hey, with you two in my corner, I've got nothing to worry about," Megan said. "Come on, group hug."

Jeb was coming out of the parsonage as she walked up the hill. His smile when he saw her left no doubt in her mind that the previous night had been real. They loved each other and did not care who knew it.

"I'm headed over to Eagle River to make some hospital visits," he said. "Do you want to ride along?"

"Can't. I'm helping Dad paint and then we have to get things ready for tonight."

He kissed her forehead as normally as if they did that sort of thing all the time. Megan could not disguise her pleasure or her discomfort.

"Get used to it," he said and kissed her again. "I'll be back after lunch to help with the party, okay?"

"Bye."

"Love you," he called and then grinned. "Really like saying that," he shouted as he drove off.

Megan was still smiling as she rounded the corner of the church and saw Owen wrestling with the extension ladder. "Dad, let me help."

"Grab that end there. That's it. Now ease it up." He pulled on the rope to extend the top of the ladder along the church wall. "Good. You want to work down here on these windows or the big one over the door there?"

"I'll go up top. You've got no business trying to balance on a ladder—not in this hot sun."

Owen grinned. "You always were a bossy little thing." He waited until she had climbed to position and then handed up a bucket of paint and a brush. "Not so much paint on the brush now," he called when she took the first stroke.

They worked in silence for nearly an hour, exchanging only whatever conversation was necessary to get the job done. When Megan had finished the trim around the large stained-glass window over the door, she came down and started working on the doors themselves.

"Dad?"

"Yeah?" His tone said he was expecting some question or comment about the work.

"I've missed you."

At first there was no response and Megan felt the familiar bonds of rejection tighten. Then he pulled a bandanna from his hip pocket and blew his nose. "Meggie, this thing with you and Jeb, I hope that works out for you. Nobody deserves a bit of happiness more than you do."

"I've been happy. I have Faith, and there's Reba and…"

"You know what I mean."

And she did. In his way he was trying to apologize.

"You'll always be part of me, Dad—part of Faith, as well."

"You've done a fine job raising that girl. You're a good mother."

"Thanks."

They worked in silence then, the air between them as thick with unspoken regrets and unanswered questions about the past as it was with the steamy humidity.

Around noon Faith walked up the lane carrying a picnic basket. "Looks good," she said. "How about taking a break for lunch? Just the three of us?"

Like a family, Megan thought. "Sure. We're done here. Let me wash out these brushes while you and Dad get things set up there in the shade."

Megan stood at the church's work sink for some time, letting the cool water run over her fingers as she stroked the brushes free of paint. There had been other times when the changes she faced seemed as momentous as those she faced now that she and Jeb were planning a future. But she could not recall one time when she had been surer that the change was for the best.

"So, Gramps, you'll have to rent a tux," Faith teased as the three of them feasted on cheese, fruit and Reba's famous pasta salad. Faith had kept the conversation going with a running commentary on the weddings she'd read about—usually those of her favorite celebrities.

"Oh, honey, I doubt we'll be that formal," Megan said.

"Why would I need a tux anyway?" Owen asked. "I've got a perfectly decent blue suit."

Faith sighed. "The men in the wedding party always wear tuxedos."

"Now don't go getting ahead of yourself," Owen said. "This is your mother's wedding, not yours, and she decides who…"

"Dad's blue suit will be perfectly fine for walking me down the aisle," Megan said, and then realized when she saw Owen's expression what she had just decided.

"Thank you, honey," he said, and concentrated on finishing the last of his lunch.

Then Megan saw the tears that had gathered at the

corners of his eyes and knew that he understood the gift she had just offered. "You're welcome, Dad."

Faith seemed oblivious to the exchange. "So then Jessica will probably be your matron of honor—she could wear blue, as well. A lighter shade, but maybe it should be an all-blue wedding—you know, like blue skies, clear sailing?"

"Actually I had someone else in mind for that role."

"But she's your best friend."

"And you're my daughter—no contest."

Faith's eyes widened with delight. "For real?"

"As long as you promise not to upstage the bride," Owen teased.

And then the three of them were laughing together, all talking at the same time and in general acting, Megan thought, like a real family.

"Ooh, look at that line of clouds," Faith said. "I hope it's not going to rain and spoil things."

Owen squinted at the sky. "I expect we'll get some rain later this afternoon. Should be fine by the time your party gets going."

But Megan wasn't so sure. The way everything was going perfectly in her life made her nervous. Experience had taught her that it was times like this when the happiness of those she cared most about was in jeopardy. "I'll clear this stuff up and take it back to the house," she said. "I just want to call Jeb. He was supposed to be back by now."

Owen and Faith exchanged a grin. "It's love, all right," Owen whispered as his granddaughter helped him to his feet and they walked back to the church together.

Chapter Fourteen

"Good thing we had the parade and fireworks yesterday," Jessica said as she carried trays of baked goods into the church basement late that afternoon. "The television said we could expect some rough weather later today and tonight. Oh, my, look what you've done to the place."

Faith and Caleb were hanging the last of the decorations and Megan was setting tables with red gingham cloths, blue napkins and centerpieces made of daisies from the field behind the church.

"Mom, Caleb and I are going out for a while, okay? Some kids are meeting at the lake for a swim."

"Sure. Jessica and I can finish up here. If it starts to rain, stay out of the water though."

"Oh, Mom," Faith groaned, and rolled her eyes.

"And stop on the way back and pick up your grandfather. He went back to the trailer for a shower and a nap."

"Got it. See you."

"Where's Jeb?" Jessica asked as she placed goodies on trays and then wrapped each in plastic.

"He was making visits at the hospital and they

brought in the Worthen boy—tractor accident. The doctors are performing surgery on his mangled leg. Jeb said he was going to stay with the family until the surgery is over, just to be sure."

"He's a good man, your Jeb."

Megan digested the sound of that. He was her Jeb now and the thought made her smile.

"Well, now look at you with that Cheshire cat grin. Does this mean there's been a change in the relationship?"

"Sorta. Kinda." Megan couldn't seem to stifle her giggle.

"Okay, give." Jessica propped one hip against a table and folded her arms.

"We're in love," Megan admitted, and her face felt as if a light had just gone on inside her.

"Do tell. That, my dear, is not news to anyone with eyes."

"You know what I mean."

"Oh, you mean you and Jeb actually have faced the music and stated the fact out loud? To each other?"

Megan nodded. She could not seem to stop smiling. But then she had a thought that dampened her good mood immediately. "I'm sure not everyone in town is going to think this is exactly a match made in heaven."

Jessica snorted. "And so what? You and Jeb are marrying each other, not one of them. You are getting married?"

"Well, yeah, I guess. I mean, eventually. Oh, Jess, it's all so new. Can't we just enjoy this moment before we rush into the next?"

Jessica pushed herself off the table and held out her arms. "You're right."

The two friends hugged each other.

"I am so glad to have you back in my life, Meggie," Jessica whispered. "My brother was such an idiot to leave you."

"Oh, Jess, I forgave Danny long ago. I just always worried about the effect on Faith."

Jessica returned to her work on the trays. "And now?"

"After Owen came back, I thought a lot about Faith and Danny. Jeb even suggested I set up a meeting between them."

"I'm not sure Dan could handle that."

"Not an issue. You see, I realized that it's not my call. Danny knows how to be in touch with Faith should he ever want to make that move, and there's not much I could do to stop him."

"Not likely he'll ever work up that kind of nerve," Jessica said.

"No, but I decided to even the playing field. I told Faith that if she ever wanted to make contact with her father, all she had to do was say so and we'd make that happen. You would help me, right?"

Jessica's hand hovered above the last lemon square and then, as she set it gently in the very center of the platter, she nodded. "I would. Not just for Faith, but for my brother. My prayer is that someday he will have a chance to know that his biggest success in life may be bringing that kid into the world."

It was nearly seven and raining by the time Jeb left the hospital. The Worthen boy had made it through surgery and the doctors had reported that his prognosis was excellent for a full recovery. "A bit of a limp," the doctor had said, "but nothing that will hamper him doing whatever he wants to do."

Jeb made a dash for his car just as the skies opened up and the drizzle became a downpour. In the background he could hear the sirens sounding a tornado watch, meaning conditions were right for a tornado to form, but none had yet been spotted.

Jeb flicked open his cell to call Megan and let her know he was on his way back, but service—always questionable in this area—was nonexistent. No matter. He'd be back home within the hour, even with the weather.

Home, he thought as he backed out of the parking space. How quickly the little village of Singing Springs and its people had come to mean that to him. *No, it's more than the town and the good people who live there, God. It's Megan. You sent her into my life and for the first time since the accident I can see a life for myself that goes beyond how I'll earn a living. You have given me a family again. Thank You. Thank You. Thank You. Inadequate words, but from my heart.*

He flicked on the radio and drummed his fingers on the steering wheel in time to the music, thinking about Faith and how best to build a relationship with the girl. He wasn't her father, and yet in time maybe she would come to think of him in that role—to trust him to be there for her. He envisioned going with Megan and Faith to tour colleges. The three of them. A family. God had given him a new chance to get things right this time and he would not waste that opportunity.

A crack of thunder and flash of lightning made him press down harder on the accelerator, anxious to see Megan and Faith. Anxious to get started on this life God had given him.

* * *

"It's late in the season for that siren to be screaming," Reba announced as she hustled into the church basement from the driving rain.

"I think we might have a bigger turnout than expected." Pete Burbank observed the size of the crowd already gathering in the youth center. "Ever since we built that shelter, folks hear that siren and come right here."

Megan remembered the terrible year when the little town of Barneveld had been leveled by a tornado that had winds up to three hundred miles per hour and stayed on the ground for nearly an hour. After that, communities throughout the state had started to take a serious look at their preparedness for just such a disaster. That's when the town council had decided that the sturdiest building around was the Singing Springs Memorial Chapel. Its walls were nearly a foot thick and it was set against a hillside that made a perfect location for a shelter.

"I'd best check the supplies in there," Reba said. "Meggie, you want to give me a hand?"

"I'll come, Reba," Jessica offered. "Megan's a little worried about Faith and Owen," she confided as the two women walked to the back of the hall.

Megan saw Reba start to turn back. "I'm sure they're fine," she said, pasting on what she hoped was a confident smile. "Probably had to take the long way round, with all this rain."

"Where's Jeb?" Reba asked.

"Probably still at the hospital. Go on, now. I'll let you know the minute they all get here."

Megan remained by the door, halfheartedly greeting

each new arrival, disappointed that it wasn't Faith, Owen or Jeb.

"Dad!" she cried when he was fairly blown into the church, accompanied by a crack of thunder too close for comfort. "Are you all right?"

"Right as that rain," he muttered. "I brought extra batteries for the lights in the shelter."

Owen Osbourne had helped build that shelter, Megan remembered suddenly. In those days—before her mother had left them—Owen had been the chief of the volunteer fire department as well as a successful attorney. Everyone had looked up to him, and Megan suddenly remembered how proud she had felt to be his daughter.

Daughter.

She turned back to the door, shut tight now. "Where's Faith?" she asked.

Owen blinked at her, his expression stating clearly that he had no idea.

"She was supposed to come get you—she and Caleb—and then all of you would come here together."

"Mike brought me in. He dropped me off here and went on over to the fire station. Are you telling me our Faith is out there somewhere? In this?"

"I don't know, Dad," Megan said as she pulled on a heavy slicker one of the men had left by the door. "But I intend to find her."

She was halfway out the door when Owen grabbed her arm. "Let me go."

"You stay here and wait for Jeb. Tell him I headed for the lake road—the kids went swimming earlier."

"Call him on your cell," Owen said.

"I tried. It went straight to voice mail. He must be out of range." As if to prove her point the lights in the church flickered, went dark and then came on again. "I'll be fine, Dad."

She felt his fingers slip off the vinyl of the slicker and she made a dash for her car. "Please let it start," she prayed and when it did, she whispered, "Thank You."

Driving north through town she almost missed the turn to the lake road. The rain was coming down in sheets now and her wipers were of little use, so she put the side window down and leaned out. "Faith!" she shouted, and felt the sound flung back at her by the wind. Her child would never hear her in this.

The minute Jeb entered the church basement he knew something was wrong—more than just the danger of the weather outside.

"Faith's missing and Meggie went to find her," Owen reported. "I tried to…"

Jeb fought against his fury that Megan's father had failed to stop her. The truth was that Owen Osbourne was a weak man, if history was any measure. Jeb marveled at the strength Megan had developed over the years. She sure hadn't had much of a parental example to inspire her. "Any idea which way she went?"

"She said to tell you she was going to circle the lake. The kids were swimming earlier and that's also where the Armstrong kid lives. I expect she plans to start with him."

Jeb zipped up his jacket and pulled up the hood. "Get everyone inside the shelter now, Owen," he instructed. "The siren was sounding a watch when I drove up. There's been a tornado spotted somewhere in the area and we don't want to take any chances."

"I'll…"

The church door blew open with a bang.

"Caleb?" It took a moment for Jeb to be sure. The young man was wearing an old camouflage rain suit and his face was half-hidden by the hood. When Caleb pushed it back with an impatient swipe, Jeb saw a face filled with panic. "What's happened?"

"Is Faith here?" Caleb demanded, ignoring Jeb's question. When both Owen and Jeb shook their heads, the boy's face collapsed into abject despair and he looked as if he might be sick any moment.

"Come over here and sit down," Jeb said, leading Caleb to the closest bench. "We thought Faith would be with you."

"She was. We had an argument and she started walking back to town. My brother, Kyle, told me to go home and cool off and he took off after her."

At that, the boy just stopped talking and stared at the floor. Then Jeb saw that he was crying. He put his hand on Caleb's back. "What else?"

"I went home, but that was over an hour ago, so I drove over here figuring Faith refused to let Kyle bring her back to our folks' place. But she's not here, either?"

"No. Where are your parents?"

"They drove over to Eagle River for a party. They're not due back until late tonight."

"Now, think," Jeb ordered. "Is there any chance you passed Kyle on the way here?"

Caleb shrugged, then broke down in sobs. "He'd been drinking, Rev Jeb. I mean, he's always drinking, but if anything's happened to Faith it's going to be my fault—my stupid ego."

Jeb exchanged a look with Owen across the boy's back. "You okay with this," Jeb mouthed, nodding at the heartbroken kid, and Owen nodded.

"Go find my girls, Jeb. I got things covered here," he said, placing his hand on Caleb's shoulder. "Now, before Rev Jeb goes out to clean up this mess you and your brother have made, is there anything else you can think of that might help him find my granddaughter?"

Caleb just slowly shook his head from side to side and kept on crying.

"Get him and the others in the shelter," Jeb shouted when he opened the door, and the shrill call of the warning siren filled the church.

An earsplitting crack of thunder followed a shot of lightning that lit the nearly black sky like daylight, all in the few seconds it took Jeb to run from the church to his car. *Show me the way,* he prayed. *Please don't let them be harmed. Not now when we've just found each other. Not now when I thought You were giving me a second chance to get it right this time.*

He was grateful for four-wheel drive as he roared down the lane past the deserted inn. He was certain that Reba had gotten every guest up to the church to wait out the storm in the shelter. Singing Springs was like a ghost town. No traffic and no sign of life. He turned onto the lake road, spraying water in a wave that a surfer might envy as he did so.

He was driving directly into the storm now and, even with his wipers on high, he could barely see. He slowed down, straining to identify every shadow and shape ahead. He was halfway around the lake road already and had seen no signs of either Megan's old sedan or the Armstrong kid's sports car. *Where are they? Please, show me the way.*

He had made the turn at the far end of the lake onto the road that would take him past the lake homes on the other side when he thought he saw something.

* * *

Megan was soaked and still she had seen nothing. She'd stopped at the Armstrongs' summer home, but no one was there. Caleb's mother had ordered a cake to donate for the party, telling Megan that she and her husband would be in Eagle River all day and evening. Caleb's car was gone, and there was no sign of his brother's sports car, either. Although something that expensive might well be inside the three-car garage attached to the enormous log home.

Leaving the car running and the flashers illuminated in case someone came barreling down the drive, Megan raced up to the front entrance and hammered on the door. When there was no answer she walked the length of the porch, peering in windows and shouting "Hello!" at the top of her lungs. But she was no match for the storm's fury. Her cries were answered only by thunderclaps and the howling wind and pelting rain.

She raced back down the stairs and slid into her car. The cloth seat was soaked because she'd left the window down. *Where is she? Please help me. I can't find my daughter! Oh, I wish Jeb were here. He would know what to do.*

She forced herself to breathe deeply and let it out slowly as she rested her forehead on the steering wheel and tried to think of where to look next. Suddenly her head shot up and her eyes widened. *The cave. Why didn't I think of it before?*

She thrust the car into gear, rolled down the drive and turned back the way she had come. The cave wasn't really a cave at all. Rather it was a hollowed-out place set into the rocky hillside above the lake where loggers had worked over a century ago. More recently—even in Megan's youth—it had become a favorite place for kids to go when they didn't want adults to know what they were up to. She and Danny had gone there more than once that summer.

That summer when we thought we were in love, she recalled. And as she tried to hold the car on the road and move as fast as possible, Megan prayed that her daughter had not fallen for the oldest trick in the teenage boy's book—*if you love me, you'll...*

The tires spun as she whipped the car onto the overgrown and rutted lane. Water ran toward her like a creek, obliterating the ruts and forcing her to slow to a crawl. She peered through the darkness of a storm-drenched dusk and saw, not Caleb's car, but the sports car belonging to his brother.

She had barely cut the motor before she was outside her car and running for Kyle's. She wrenched open the door and bent to peer inside.

Kyle was slumped against the steering wheel. He was snoring loudly and there was no sign of Faith.

Chapter Fifteen

"What have you done with my daughter?" Megan shouted as she shook the young man hard. She refused to use the question that had sprung immediately to mind: what have you done *to* my daughter?

The interior of the car reeked of alcohol, a smell that Megan thought she had successfully banished from her memory for all time once her father had left for good. But it hit her in the face with as much force as the rain had blasted her all afternoon. She squeezed her eyes shut and shook Kyle again. "Where is she?"

Kyle mumbled something and shrugged her off. That's when Megan saw her daughter's purse lying on the floor and noticed that the passenger door was open.

"Faith!" she screamed, running around the car and climbing over a tangle of wild raspberry vines to reach the passenger side. *Nothing.*

"Faith?" This time her voice cracked and the sound was no more than a whimper. *Oh, please let her be all right.* Megan repeated this mantra for several moments and then realized that everything around her had gone silent. The rain had slackened to a drizzle, the wind was calm and the clouds that rolled across the sky cast an eerie greenish-yellow glow.

"Tornado," Megan whispered. She stumbled to her feet and back around to where Kyle was now staring at his surroundings as if trying to figure out where he was.

"Get out of that car now," Megan ordered. She started up the barely visible path that led to the shelter loggers had once dug into the hillside and the teen population of Singing Springs had maintained ever since. "Come on. Move," she called, as Kyle staggered out of the vehicle and started to follow her.

"Mom?"

Megan looked up and for a moment thought she must have conjured Faith's image, so desperate was she to see her daughter safe and sound. But the figure running toward her was no mirage. Megan held out her arms and caught Faith in a bear hug. "We have to get to the shelter," she said.

"I know. I went there when I heard the siren change from watch to warning."

"But you came back because you heard me calling you?"

"No." She glanced back at Kyle with disgust. "When things got so calm and the sky turned that putrid green color I figured I'd better get him up to the shelter if I could. Much as I can't stand him, he was going to be a sitting duck if a tornado comes through here."

"Oh, honey, you are such a good person." Megan wrapped her arm around her daughter's shoulder as they climbed up an even narrower path that led over the rise and down to the shelter. She glanced back to be sure that Kyle was still following them, but he'd stopped on the trail and was staring at something in the western sky.

Megan followed his gaze just as the wind began to pick up again and debris from the forest floor began swirling around their feet. In the sky to the west she saw a row of black thunderclouds, and dropping out of one of them was the unmistakable funnel of a tornado. "Go," she cried, pushing Faith ahead of her then turning back to Kyle.

She grabbed the young man's hand. "Tornado," she mouthed and was relieved to see some semblance of sobriety register in his bloodshot eyes. "Let's go."

Once again the sky had gone black as midnight, and Megan had trouble seeing the way as she pulled Kyle along with her. *Stupid to leave the flashlight in the car,* she thought, and her anger at herself served to fuel her strength as she dragged Kyle along, oblivious to his cries of protest when he ran into brush and thorns.

"Oh, stop being such a baby," she ordered, turning to glance back at him and failing to see the fallen tree that blocked their way.

"Mom!" was the last thing she heard as she went down hard and felt her forehead collide with what could only be one of several granite boulders that pocked the hillside.

Jeb had driven almost the entire circle of the lake, stopping at houses along the way to see if Megan and Faith had taken shelter there. There'd been no sign of them and now the winds and rain had calmed and the sky was definitely lighter. He glanced at his watch. *Seven-forty.* Other than a slight yellowish cast, the sky looked normal. *Maybe it's over,* he thought and turned on the radio.

Through the static he heard the otherworldly voice of the emergency services announcer. "Series of tornadoes traveling east-northeast across Wisconsin. Seek shelter immediately. Tornado sighted two miles south-west of Singing Springs…."

Jeb pulled onto a narrow, overgrown side road and got out to scan the sky to the west. The clouds were black and thick and rolling toward him, picking up speed and debris as they came.

Jeb sheltered his face with his forearm and the hood of the slicker. He knew he had to get away from his car but there was no ditch he could use to ride out the storm. Scanning his surroundings, he thought he heard shouts. And then a flash of lightning revealed a split-second glimpse of Megan's old car, flashers blinking weakly.

Without further thought for anything other than finding Megan before it was too late, Jeb started to run toward the faltering amber light. The closer he got, the harder he prayed. *Please let her be all right. Let her have found Faith and together let us find shelter from the storm so we can start a new life together. Please, God. Whatever bargain Megan has made with You this time, let it be one You have heard.*

Megan's car doors were open and the interior was unoccupied, as was the sports car parked a few feet away. Ahead was a hillside and Jeb caught a glimpse of movement.

"Megan," he bellowed at the top of his lungs.

"Rev Jeb!"

Faith.

Jeb scrambled up the hillside. What was the kid doing out here in the middle of nowhere with a tornado coming? "Seek shelter," he shouted. "Now."

Easier said than done, Jeb thought, as he clawed his way up the slippery slope of the hill.

"Oh, Rev Jeb," Faith cried when she saw him. "It's

my mom. She fell and hit her head and there's blood and I'm afraid to move her and…"

Jeb found his footing and knelt next to Megan, who moaned as he touched her face. "She's coming around," he said. "We have to get out of here. Is that Kyle?" He jerked his head in the direction of a figure doubled over and retching.

"He's pathetic," Faith said with disgust. "There's an old logger's shelter just over the rise there. That's where we were headed when Mom fell."

Jeb handed Faith the flashlight from his pocket and scooped Megan into his arms. "Lead the way," he told the girl. "Kyle Armstrong," he shouted. "Move. Now."

His mind went into overdrive, considering the situation from every possible angle as he had when he'd been running the corporation.

"He's not coming," Faith shouted, and hesitated.

"Go," Jeb ordered. "I'll come back for him."

Faith scurried forward and suddenly disappeared over a rise. Jeb followed and in seconds they had reached the man-made cave. He quickly surveyed the situation. The solid rock wall that shaped the place would take the brunt of the storm's force if they sustained a direct hit, and a second boulder at the entrance would be another barrier for protection. "Sit there," he instructed, pointing to the narrow passage between the rock wall and the boulder. He was thankful that Faith did not question him. When she was crouched next to the large boulder, he laid Megan down so that her head rested on Faith's lap. "Cover your head with your arms and bend forward to cover your mother."

Faith nodded and did exactly as he asked. Jeb

grabbed the flashlight and turned just as Kyle stumbled into the enclosure.

"I'm so sorry," he blubbered, bracing both palms flat against the boulder that blocked the entrance.

"Save it," Jeb snapped, barely able to control his fury at the young man. "Sit over here, cover your head with your arms and brace yourself." Just as Jeb squeezed in next to Faith and Megan, sheltering them both with his arms and body, hail the size of golf balls bounced off the rocks.

Then in the distance they heard a roar coming closer. "It really does sound like an oncoming train," Jeb heard Faith say, and at that same moment he felt the girl's hand snake into his and hold on tight.

Megan's eyes were squeezed shut against the noise of destruction that accompanied the tornado. Outside they heard trees crack and splinter as if someone had set a charge of dynamite at their core. Whirlwinds of leaves, pine cones, sticks and small fist-size rocks whipped through the narrow passage and then out again. Fragments of fallen trees made their way past the protective barricade of the boulder and showered them with debris. Megan pulled Faith closer.

Her head was throbbing, though whether that was from the injury of her fall or the incredible pressure of the air around them, she could not have said. All she knew was that she felt as if she might explode into a thousand pieces like the trees outside or the glass and wood of the homes and businesses across the lake if the tornado struck Singing Springs.

She prayed that her father and Reba and Jessica and her family and all her friends and neighbors were safe. She prayed for those people she did not know who might suffer in the storm. She prayed for the patience to hear Kyle out once he tried to explain how her daughter had come to be in such a dangerous situation in the first place.

But most of all she prayed for the future she had imagined sharing with Jeb—a future where at long last she and Faith would have a real home, be a real family and she would know the true love she had dreamed of all her life.

Gradually she became aware that the storm had passed and lost power over the lake. She opened her eyes. It was still dark inside the shelter and yet the sky beyond the entrance seemed lighter—a normal summer's dusk. It seemed like hours since she'd left the church to search for Faith, but her watch told her that barely an hour had passed.

"You okay?" Jeb's breath fanned her face as he ran his fingers gently over her forehead.

"Yeah. You?"

"Never better."

Faith squirmed between them to raise her head and look out. "It's over, right?"

"It's over," Jeb assured her, "but it looks like it might take us a while to get back to the cars—that is, if the cars are still there." He pointed toward the giant tree that had fallen across the entrance. "Any ideas?" He looked at both women and then over at Kyle.

"I think I might be able to squeeze through those branches there, sir, and then I could go for help," Kyle offered, still slightly slurring his words. But he was sobering up, and he had always been respectful and courteous when he wasn't drinking.

"You stay here with Mom, Rev Jeb," Faith said, "in

case—you know—she passes out or something from loss of blood."

"It's a scratch and a bump," Megan protested. "I am perfectly capable of…" But when she tried to get to her feet a wave of dizziness washed over her, forcing her to sit down again. "Or not," she admitted with a weak smile.

"Keys," Faith said, holding out her hand.

"Left mine in the car," Jeb said.

"Me, too," Megan admitted.

Faith turned to Kyle, hand extended.

"Oh, no way," he protested. "You are not driving my car. In fact, you aren't driving, period. You're not old enough."

"I was old enough for you to make a pass at me," Faith told him, her eyes locked on his until he had the decency to look away. "And I have my learner's permit. And I have no record of DUIs. How's your record, Kyle?" she asked sweetly.

"I…I'm…"

"You're an egotistical creep and well on your way to being a drunk," Faith continued. "Now we can keep on debating this or you can ride shotgun so that I'm not breaking the law by driving into town for help. Either way I am so outta here."

Megan watched Faith wriggle through an opening in the branches that seemed too small for a cat, much less her suddenly grown-up daughter. She had never been more proud of the child in her life. *Thank You, God.*

Kyle was still standing with his mouth open. "Well, I'll be," the young man finally muttered, and followed Faith's path through the fallen tree.

"Do you think she'll be all right?" Megan was having

second thoughts about not asking Jeb to go for help and keeping Faith close by.

Jeb grinned. "She's her mother's daughter to the core. She'll be fine." He knelt next to Megan. "You're the one we have to worry about. That's a nasty bump you got there." He ran his thumb over her forehead, then down her temple to caress her cheek. "Do you have any idea how worried I was? What if something had happened to you?"

Megan saw more than concern in the way he looked at her. She realized that he had been truly frightened. And why not?

"Jeb, I'm right here."

He rested his forehead against hers. "I was so afraid of losing you," he admitted. "Both of you."

They kissed, each reaching for the other to offer love and reassurance.

"You know what I was thinking?" Jeb asked a minute later as they leaned against the shelter wall and heard nothing but the birds singing and the soft breeze rustling through the trees.

"What?"

"I was thinking that—if you're willing—why not get married right away? Why wait?"

Megan was certain that he was reacting to the trauma of the day. Once they were back in town and could see that everyone was all right, he would regret such a rash offer. "Jeb, you don't have to marry me to be sure I'm going to be here. I mean, don't you want to—you know—date awhile and see how that goes?"

"We're not kids, Megan. We both know what's at stake in a relationship like ours, and no amount of time spent testing the waters is going to change that. I'm thinking we should just dive right in and get started on what I believe is going to be a spectacular life for the two of us and Faith." His eyes brightened with understanding. "That's it, isn't it? You want to give Faith time to adjust to the idea."

"I want to give *you* time, Jeb."

"I don't need time. I need you. Since I met you I've come to realize how much I had put my life on hold after the accident. Oh, sure, I made big changes, but they were more external. Until you came along and I began to…to feel again. That's when I realized that leaving the business world and getting my divinity degree—those were just stepping stones to this—to us."

"I do love you," Megan said, feeling suddenly shy yet more sure than she'd ever been of anything in her life. "I know now that the jolt of recognition I felt that first Sunday you took the pulpit was God's tap on the shoulder."

Jeb pulled her into his arms. "And what was God telling you?"

"I thought He was reminding me that I had gotten too comfortable with my past, that living here in Singing Springs, where everyone knew my story and had moved on, had become too safe. I thought He had sent you to remind me that there would always be new people who would hear the story of my past and make their own judgment."

"I never judged you, Megan."

"I know, and that confused me for a while. You were so different from Reverend Dunhill. I mean, it had never occurred to me that my minister might also be my friend…and more."

"Much more." Jeb kissed her temple. "Marry me, Megan."

Megan closed her eyes for a minute, silently praying

that what she wanted more than anything in her life was also God's will for her. "Yes," she whispered and, realizing she'd spoken aloud, she lifted her face to his and grinned. "Yes," she shouted, the sound bouncing off the hard stone surrounding them. She flung her arms around Jeb. "Tomorrow, next week, next year."

Their joyous laughter was interrupted by the approach of townspeople with lamps and chain saws. "You two okay?" Pete Burbank called.

"Couldn't be better," Jeb assured him. "Now get us out of here."

Chapter Sixteen

Megan's high spirits were dampened by the reality of
the storm's aftermath. Their first indication of the extent
of the damage was the large tree that had fallen on
Kyle's sports car, crushing it as if it were made of paper.
Megan couldn't suppress the shudder that ran through
her at the idea that Faith could have been in that car.

The lake road itself was littered with branches and
debris. Jeb reached over and held her hand. "Mike
Caspin said nobody was hurt, Megan."

"And I'm thankful for that, but, Jeb, what about their
homes and businesses? What if the inn or Reba's house
or the church…"

"Shh… It will all work out," he assured her. "Everyone will pull together as they always do."

He turned onto the main road and Megan breathed a
sigh of relief when she saw only minor damage—a door
ripped askew here, some broken glass there and roof
tiles littering the street in several places. "It doesn't
look as bad as it was back there," she said as they passed
people already starting to clean up.

"I expect the thing blew itself out once it was over the lake, and that saved the town from extensive damage." He turned onto the lane that led them past the inn and up to the parsonage and church.

Megan sat forward, scanning each structure for damage, and when she saw Reba and Faith putting the inn's rocking chairs back in place on the porch, she practically leaped from the car before Jeb could bring it to a stop.

"Mom!" Faith cried, setting a chair down and running to meet them. "Are you okay?"

"Just a nasty bruise on this hard head of mine. How about you?"

"Couple of scratches from climbing around in the cave up there."

Mother and daughter held one another at arm's length as if to reassure themselves that both had indeed survived the storm. Then Megan pulled Faith close and hugged her until the girl was laughing. "Mom, I need to breathe."

Megan loosened her hold as the images of how differently this all might have played out raced through her mind once again. "Where's Kyle?" she asked.

"Uh-oh, you're wearing your got-to-protect-my-cub face."

"Where is he?"

"Nursing a black eye and bloody nose," Faith said, pointing toward a hunched figure on the steps of the church. "Caleb belted him good, and if he hadn't I think Gramps might have. He was so ticked off."

By this time Reba had hobbled down the porch steps, and Jeb, who had hung back to give mother and daughter time, stepped forward.

"You get yourself up to the house and get some ice

on that bump, missy," Reba ordered. Her snappishness was a clear indication that she had been frightened and now needed to take action.

"Yes, ma'am," Megan said, as she took the older woman's arm and headed back to the house.

"Faith, could I talk to you a moment?" Jeb asked when Faith started to follow them.

The girl eyed him with her usual polite but distant smile. "Sure."

All around them people were scurrying around, cleaning up after the storm, calling out greetings to those they hadn't seen since before the storm, and—in a few cases—clearly waiting for Jeb to take charge at the church.

"I'll be there in a few minutes," he called when Rick Epstein shouted a question about boarding up some broken windows. Jeb turned his attention back to Faith. "Could we walk down to the pier?"

Her eyes narrowed. "I wasn't drinking, Rev Jeb. The others were, but I promised Mom, and besides…"

"This isn't a lecture or sermon, Faith. I need to ask you something, okay?"

Curious now, Faith walked with him to the pier.

"Ever skip a rock?" Jeb asked, scooping up a handful of stones from the side of the road. He was suddenly nervous in the presence of this strong-willed girl who he hoped one day might think of him as her father.

"That's the big question?"

"No. It's small talk," he admitted, skipping a stone across the water and then offering her one from his collection.

She took it and skipped it expertly.

"Wow. Impressive," he said, and meant it.

"Thanks." She took another stone from his hand and skipped it. "Look, if this is about you dating Mom, I have no objections. You make her happy and that's a good thing."

"And what if I didn't want to date her? What if I wanted to marry her?"

Faith's third stone plopped and sank on the first bounce. "That's not news."

"What if we'd decided to marry as soon as possible— like maybe in a week or so?"

That got her attention. "Are you serious? I thought the plan was to wait until I graduated or at least…"

"Look, Faith, one thing I've figured out in my short time as a minister is that God has a way of tapping us on the shoulder from time to time, reminding us that life on this planet is short and He expects us to make the most of it. What I'm asking, Faith, is your blessing for your mom and me to marry—soon."

Instead of answering, Faith sat down on the edge of the pier, her feet dangling over the water. "You had a wife and a daughter." It wasn't a question.

"I did."

"Mom says your daughter would have been about my age."

"A year or so younger."

"You must miss them both."

Jeb began to see where this was going, so he sat next to her without touching her. "I will always miss them, Faith. But they aren't coming back. This isn't about trying to replace them. Your mother is nothing at all like my late wife and you are nothing like my daughter—and I am not at all the man I was when they were part of my life."

"Still…"

"I think your mom deserves some real happiness—the kind that comes wrapped in the love of a man who respects her and sees a future with her that could make such a difference. I think I can offer her that, and I already know what she gives to me."

Faith's hair fell across her face. "What?"

"She makes my heart sing in ways it hasn't in a very long time—even long before my wife and daughter died. And I think because she has known her own pain, she understands the pain of others."

Several minutes passed and Jeb had to fight his instinct to keep stating his case as he would have in a business situation.

"Do I have to call you Dad?"

"Well, the way you phrased that tells me you'd rather not, and that's fine with me."

"Because I have a dad." Faith continued as if he hadn't spoken. "He doesn't seem to want me, but he's out there and Mom told me I could make my own choice about when or even whether to contact him." She swiped at tears and Jeb risked touching her shoulder.

Instead of jerking away as he might have expected, she collapsed against him, her tears coming in earnest now. "He just doesn't know you," Jeb said, wrapping his arm around her. "And when and if you decide to contact him, he's going to regret all the time he let pass without knowing you. In the meantime, you've got your grandfather."

"And you," she whispered.

"And me," Jeb assured her.

They decided on an outdoor wedding in Reba's flower garden next to the inn—a decision that Megan had second thoughts about when she came downstairs one morning and found Reba surrounded by crude drawings and pictures of massive floral displays.

"Containers," she announced. "That's the answer. With containers, you can have the color palette and design you want. I've already contacted Margie Caspin and she's agreed to let us dig some of her perennials. Question is whether or not they'll hold up. Well, with stakes and enough water, we can make them work. Now then…"

"Reba, this looks like a lot of work, and where are you going to get containers this size?"

"They have some at the garden center in Eagle River."

"But they'll cost a fortune."

"Not at all. I spoke to the owner and suggested that they could launch a whole new facet of their business by agreeing to set up this wedding on a rental basis."

"Still…"

"Oh, honey, let me give you and Jeb this, okay?"

Megan hesitated.

"The more you learn to say yes, the better your life is going to be, missy," Reba warned.

"Yes," Megan said, her expression a mask of pain. Then she grinned. "Yes, thank you," she said and hugged Reba.

"Mom?" Faith shouted from outside as a car horn tooted. "Are you coming or what?"

"Jessica's taking us shopping for a gown and maid of honor dress," Megan reminded Reba. "Promise me you won't try digging up anything until we get back, okay?" She kissed Reba's forehead and grabbed her purse. "Coming!"

Chapter Seventeen

Megan was determined to remember every detail of
her wedding day, but it had held so many surprises that
she knew it would be some time before the full impact
of all the ways her life had changed hit her.

The day had begun with Owen's announcement as the
two of them sat together in the back of the empty church
just hours before the guests were scheduled to arrive.

"I was thinking about that Armstrong kid," he said.
"The older boy. Seems to me he's on a path to self-
destruction."

"I understand that his parents have taken him back
to Milwaukee and admitted him to a clinic for alcohol
abuse," Megan said.

"That's a start. But I was talking to Jeb last night, and
he suggested there were others in town who might
benefit from getting some help."

Megan thought about the rumors surrounding at least
half a dozen people who lived in the area. "Probably,"
she admitted.

"Jeb thought that he and I might start an AA group

at the church—put the word out and see if anybody shows up."

That got Megan's full attention. She sat down opposite her father and took his hand. "Dad, that's a wonderful idea, don't you think?"

Owen shrugged. "Jeb seems to think that folks would connect with my experience, and I have to say that finding an AA meeting most everywhere I went helped keep me sober these last four years." He looked at Megan. "Do you think I could do it—help somebody else?"

"I know you can."

Owen smiled. "It would be a way of leaving something behind—something you and Faith could take pride in."

Jeb had taken Megan and Owen to see a specialist in Chicago and the news had not been good. Short of a transplant, there was little hope that Owen would make it past another couple of years, at best.

"Doctors don't know everything," Megan said, her voice strained as she tried to force out the words around the lump in her throat.

"No, and maybe God will send us a miracle, but in the meantime, nothing wrong with putting my house in order. So, what do you think?"

"I just wish…"

Owen cupped her cheek. "No more wishing, child. What do you think about the AA meeting idea?"

"I think Jeb knows a winner when he sees one. Go for it, Dad, but either way know this—I am so proud of the way you turned your life around, and I am so thankful that you decided to come back here so I could know that."

"Want to know who inspired me?"

"God?"

"You. Whatever good I may have time to do in this life, nothing will hold a candle to the good your mother and I did when we had you."

He fumbled in his pocket and pulled out an envelope that looked as if it had been lost at the post office for decades. "I had forgotten about this, Megan, until the other day when Jon Barnsworth stopped me in the bank and asked that I come to his office."

"What is it?" Megan hesitated to take the envelope, suddenly terrified that it might change everything.

"When your mother left me, she left this for you. I was supposed to give it to you when you were eighteen, but by then I was gone and you had Faith and, well, I was so pickled I forgot all about it."

"How did Mr. Barnsworth get it?"

"I had put this in a small safe-deposit box I had at the bank. When the rent on the box went unpaid for a couple of years a bank employee was told to empty the box. She brought this to Barnsworth and he just held on to it. Then with the passing of time he forgot about it as well, until I came back to town." He laid the envelope on the table. "It's yours if you want it."

The same looped handwriting that Megan had studied in the front of her childhood books had bled across the thick rose-colored parchment envelope.

"It's from her."

Owen nodded. "Maybe it's unfair to give it to you today, of all days, but I want you to start this life with Jeb without anything missing from your past. You can open it and read it, or toss it in the trash. Your choice."

Megan stared at the envelope for a long moment as memories triggered by the strange yet familiar scrawl assailed her. In what seemed like slow motion she slid her thumb under the flap. It gave easily, the glue having long since dried out.

There were two matching sheets of paper inside.

"Do you know what it says?" she asked.

"No. You want to read it to me, fine. If not, I'll leave you to it."

"Stay, Dad. This may be the answer we've both waited a lifetime to hear."

Owen settled back in the pew, his arms folded across his chest as Megan unfolded the letter.

"'My darling Megan.'" Her voice cracked and she cleared her throat impatiently. "'There are no words to explain what I'll have done by the time you read this. And there is no way I can find to not hurt you and your father in what I am doing. Someday I hope you will understand why. The truth is that I don't think I can do this anymore. I thought when I met your father that love would conquer everything, but the truth is that I want so much more than a life in Singing Springs. The very idea that I might never have the chance to follow my dreams scares me beyond anything I can imagine. And I know how selfish that must sound, but perhaps when you are my age you will understand because you will have followed dreams of your own. My wish for you is that you find everything you want in this life—happiness, success in whatever you choose to do and the love of a man as devoted and decent and caring as your father. Perhaps one day we will see each other again, but if that day never comes I will understand. This is the most difficult decision I will ever make, Megan, and if it is the wrong decision then God forgive me. All my love forever, Mom.'"

Megan clutched the paper as the storm of unacknowledged feelings rocketed through her. Anger, hostility, anguish, resentment gradually gave way to sorrow for a woman so deeply self-centered that she had knowingly turned her back on the love of a man devoted to her and of a child who had once thought the sun rose and set in her.

She folded the pages precisely and returned them to the envelope.

"Can you forgive her?" Owen asked after a long moment.

"Can you?"

He nodded. "That's why I went to California. Once I realized that I had destroyed my life and a good deal of yours by blaming myself, I had to see for myself how it had all turned out for her."

"And?"

"She never knew I was there."

"But I thought…"

"She's got a family out there, Megan. Husband, grown kids and three grandchildren. She dotes on them and she's quite the social leader in San Diego—heading up all sorts of charity events and such. From what I was able to find out, she traveled quite a bit when she first left, moved from one job to the next and finally married her boss—a real estate tycoon."

"Oh, Dad, I'm so sorry."

"I'm not. She was right. I knew early on that she wasn't happy, but I had my work here and thought in time… Jeb was telling me that he thought that way too when he was married before. 'The danger of believing in someday' is what Jeb called it."

Megan waited for tears that did not come. Instead she felt a sense of peace, of closure. Her mother had made choices as Megan had. Whether or not her mother's had been guided by God's grace she couldn't say, but she knew that hers had. Every painful and joyous moment of her life had been leading her to this day. She had never been surer of anything in her life.

"Dad?"

"Yeah."

"Ready to walk me down the aisle?"

Owen hugged her hard as the letter slipped from her grasp. "Nothing would give me greater pleasure," he assured her.

Reba insisted that it was bad luck for the groom to see his bride the day of the wedding and stationed herself on the front porch of the inn. There she had the best view of the church and parsonage and could oversee setting up the chairs outdoors for the wedding, as well. She had assigned Jessica the role of helping Faith get Megan ready.

"Reba's snapping at everyone," Megan told Jessica, as her friend applied the subtle makeup that she had assured Megan would simply highlight her natural beauty.

"It's the maternal thing. She's sending her chick out into a world she won't be here to oversee."

"I'm glad her daughter and family came up for this. They'll be a comfort to her."

Jessica laughed. "I'm not so sure. Seems to me her daughter is every bit as strong-willed and stubborn as Reba is. That's going to be an interesting household once they all move in together in Arizona."

"Reba will make it work," Megan said. *Just like she did for me and for Faith.* "I'm glad you and Pete are buying the inn."

Jessica paused, blush brush suspended just above Megan's cheek. "Reba hasn't talked to you yet, has she?"

"About?"

"Not my place to say. Let me just finish up here and I'll send her up." She fluffed pink color on Megan's cheekbones and stood back to admire her work. "Perfect. And stop frowning. This thing with Reba is good, and that is all I'm going to say."

Just then Faith burst into the room. "Mom? Down or up?" She flicked her long golden hair over one shoulder then bunched it into a ridiculous topknot that made Megan laugh.

"Definitely down."

Faith walked over to the mirror and smoothed out her hair. Then she looked closely at her mother. "Wow. You look fantastic, Mom."

"I'm in my bathrobe," Megan pointed out.

"The face, Mom. Look at yourself."

Megan usually avoided studying herself in mirrors, and Jessica had insisted on turning her away while she did the makeup. But now Megan looked closer and while the woman looking back at her was familiar, something was there she hadn't seen in a very long time—if ever. The woman in the mirror was radiant, not with cosmetics, but with bliss. After years of believing the best she could do was make sure Faith was secure, she was about to have some joy for herself.

Her eyes welled with tears of happiness and both Jessica and Faith made a grab for the box of tissues. "Oh, no, you don't," Jessica warned, dabbing gently at Megan's eyes. "There's no time for this. I'll go get Reba. Faith, help your mother with her dress and meet me in your room. I have an idea for your hair."

Reba knocked lightly, but entered the room before Megan could say a word. The two women stood facing each other, their expressions communicating what words were inadequate to say. Reba held out her arms and Megan went to her as she had so many times as a child, and later as a frightened teen.

"You look so beautiful," Reba choked out. Then she cleared her throat impatiently and swiped at her eyes with the back of one hand. "But you know that. Now, time is running short and this may be my only opportunity to give you my gift."

"Oh, Reba, you already gave us the flowers."

"This isn't your wedding gift, Megan. Now, sit and don't muss that pretty dress."

As always with Reba, Megan followed instructions. She perched on the edge of a chintz-covered side chair and waited. Reba removed a paper from one pocket and a pen from the other. She glanced around the room and took down one of the many books she and Stan had given Megan over the years. "You need to sign this," she instructed, setting the paper on top of the book and handing both to Megan.

"What is it?" Megan's heart skipped a beat when she realized she was looking at some sort of legal document.

"It's a bill of sale making you an equal partner with Pete and Jessica in the inn. You can be a silent partner if you like, but you will have a say in how this place is run."

"I can't afford this, Reba, and it's unfair to expect that Jeb…" Megan was well aware of the price that Reba's attorney had set on the property.

"Did I ask for payment?" She thrust the pen at Megan, but her hand started to shake. "Please don't refuse me this, Meggie," she said. "You have been like a daughter to me. You and Faith were my strength after my Stan died. I don't know how I would have kept going if it hadn't been for the two of you."

"It's too much," Megan protested.

"It's not nearly enough," Reba replied. "Make an old woman as happy as you are today."

"But Pete and Jessica…"

"Know all about this and are in perfect agreement with the plan." She tapped the paper, indicating the spot where Megan needed to sign. "I want you and Faith to have something of your own."

"Oh, Reba, I have so much. I have you and Faith and now Jeb. How could I possibly want more?"

Reba laid her hand on Megan's head. "That's the point—you never asked for anything for yourself, always making sure others would be all right. It's past time you had someone looking after you. Now, are you going to sign it or not?"

Megan scribbled her name, noticing that now it was her hand that shook. "I don't know what to say," she murmured, as she stared at the document and then handed it back to Reba.

"Yes, you do. Have I taught you nothing, young lady?"

Megan smiled. "Thank you?"

"Works like magic every time. Now, let's go get you married. I do hope that Rev Jeb has planned a decent honeymoon—you know men. Stan's idea of a honeymoon was to spend four days camping."

As they walked downstairs together, Megan understood that Reba was jabbering as much to still her own nerves as to quell any second thoughts Megan might have.

"You loved camping," Megan reminded her.

"Yes, but did I fail to mention that we were married over Thanksgiving? I thought my feet would never thaw out."

Both women were laughing as they walked out into the side yard. A few feet away, Owen was pacing and Faith was fussing with the headband of flowers that Jessica had woven into her hair.

"Let's get this show on the road," Reba said, taking charge as always. "Faith? Ring?"

Faith held up her forefinger, where she wore the wide gold band that Megan would give Jeb.

"Cue the music, Jessica. Owen, places."

Owen looked as if he might pass out at any moment so Megan placed her hand in the crook of his arm. "Ready, Dad?"

Owen nodded and, as Faith made her way down the aisle, Megan prepared to take her own walk to the altar, and caught her first glimpse of Jeb. He was wearing the same suit he'd worn that first Sunday. It struck her that they had known each other only a short time, and she couldn't help thinking that perhaps they were making a mistake—that he would realize it and regret marrying her.

And then Owen led her to the opening under the arbor and Jeb looked up. Megan searched his face for any of the same doubts she was feeling, but what she saw in his smile was not doubt or hesitation. Indeed, he took half a step forward as if he might come up the aisle and meet her halfway. Then the minister touched his arm lightly, stopping him.

Jeb nodded and remained in his place, but as Megan and Owen started down the aisle, Jeb held out his arms to her and in his eyes she saw only the unquestioning love and the shared future she had longed for all of her life.

The faces of neighbors and friends passed in a blur

as she walked to Jeb and, intertwining her fingers with his, they turned to face the minister.

"Dearly beloved…"

Jeb tightened his hand on hers and when she looked up at him, he mouthed the words she knew she would never tire of hearing. "Hello, my love."

* * * * *

Dear Reader,

I grew up in a town not unlike Singing Springs and, as in many small towns, our community had its share of scandal, gossip and ultimately forgiveness. That sense of community that borders on "family" inspired this story. By contrast I spent several years working for two major international corporations where I daily observed men and women who had put their personal lives on hold in the interest of achieving maximum success and financial security. Their mantra all too often was "someday," and frankly I always worried that their someday might never come.

The setting for this story is a favorite part of the beautiful state of Wisconsin—an area full of lakes of all sizes, wonderful evergreen forests and country roads that ooze peace and security. Of course, the state can be a magnet for tornadoes, and the one in Barneveld mentioned in the book actually happened and wiped out that entire town. But resilience is the hallmark of such communities and I am happy to say that the town has rebuilt and revived itself to thrive once again.

Finally this book is dedicated to the brave women I have sponsored through a wonderful organization helping women around the world to help themselves. The organization is Women for Women International, and my experience sponsoring "sisters" in war-torn countries has enriched my life beyond measure.

Thank you, dear reader, as always for choosing this book. You have no idea how special it is for an author to hear from readers, so I do hope you will drop me a line at P.O. Box 161, Thiensville WI 53092, or visit my Web site at www.booksbyanna.com.

All best wishes and many blessings to you and yours.

Anna Schmidt

QUESTIONS FOR DISCUSSION

1. How do you think small-town life differs from life in a city?

2. In what ways are they the same?

3. What is the path that has led Megan to this moment in her life?

4. What other paths might she have taken?

5. How else might Jeb have reacted to the tragedy in his life?

6. In what ways do you think Megan and Jeb made the right choices?

7. In what ways did their faith sustain each of them during their journey to this moment?

8. What might you have done differently in their situations?

9. Often in fiction a storm is a metaphor for what is happening to the characters. Do you see any such connection between the tornado and the characters in this story?

10. How might Megan and her friend Jessica have found a way to mend their friendship earlier?

11. What do you think might happen between Faith and her birth father?

12. In many ways this is a story about forgiveness. How many examples of forgiveness can you recall?

13. Do you think Megan has forgiven her mother by the end of the book? If not, does she need to do that?

14. In what ways do Megan and Jeb help each other find peace with their past?

15. Imagine you are meeting these characters ten years after the book ends. Where are they and what has changed?

TITLES AVAILABLE NEXT MONTH

Available June 29, 2010

THE GUARDIAN'S HONOR
The Bodine Family
Marta Perry

KLONDIKE HERO
Alaskan Bride Rush
Jillian Hart

HEART OF A COWBOY
Helping Hands Homeschooling
Margaret Daley

CATTLEMAN'S COURTSHIP
Carolyne Aarsen

WAITING OUT THE STORM
Ruth Logan Herne

BRIDE IN TRAINING
Gail Gaymer Martin

LICNM0610

LARGER-PRINT BOOKS!

GET 2 FREE
LARGER-PRINT NOVELS
PLUS 2 FREE
MYSTERY GIFTS

Larger-print novels are now available...

YES! Please send me 2 FREE LARGER-PRINT Love Inspired® novels and my 2 FREE mystery gifts (gifts are worth about $10). After receiving them, if I don't wish to receive any more books, I can return the shipping statement marked "cancel". If I don't cancel, I will receive 6 brand-new novels every month and be billed just $4.74 per book in the U.S. or $5.24 per book in Canada. That's a saving of over 20% off the cover price. It's quite a bargain! Shipping and handling is just 50¢ per book.* I understand that accepting the 2 free books and gifts places me under no obligation to buy anything. I can always return a shipment and cancel at any time. Even if I never buy another book, the two free books and gifts are mine to keep forever.

122/322 IDN E7QP

Name	(PLEASE PRINT)
Address	Apt. #
City	State/Prov.	Zip/Postal Code

Signature (if under 18, a parent or guardian must sign)

Mail to Steeple Hill Reader Service:
IN U.S.A.: P.O. Box 1867, Buffalo, NY 14240-1867
IN CANADA: P.O. Box 609, Fort Erie, Ontario L2A 5X3

Not valid to current subscribers to Love Inspired Larger-Print books.

**Are you a current subscriber to Love Inspired books
and want to receive the larger-print edition?
Call 1-800-873-8635 or visit www.morefreebooks.com.**

* Terms and prices subject to change without notice. Prices do not include applicable taxes. Sales tax applicable in N.Y. Canadian residents will be charged applicable provincial taxes and GST. Offer not valid in Quebec. This offer is limited to one order per household. All orders subject to approval. Credit or debit balances in a customer's account(s) may be offset by any other outstanding balance owed by or to the customer. Please allow 4 to 6 weeks for delivery. Offer available while quantities last.

Your Privacy: Steeple Hill Books is committed to protecting your privacy. Our Privacy Policy is available online at www.SteepleHill.com or upon request from the Reader Service. From time to time we make our lists of customers available to reputable third parties who may have a product or service of interest to you. If you would prefer we not share your name and address, please check here. ☐

Help us get it right—We strive for accurate, respectful and relevant communications. To clarify or modify your communication preferences, visit us at www.ReaderService.com/consumerchoice.

LILP10R

HARLEQUIN®

A Romance

FOR EVERY MOOD™

Spotlight on

— Heart & Home —

Heartwarming romances
where love can happen
right when you least expect it.

See the next page to enjoy a sneak peek
from Silhouette Special Edition®,
a Heart and Home series.

*Introducing McFARLANE'S PERFECT BRIDE
by* USA TODAY *bestselling author Christine Rimmer,
from Silhouette Special Edition®.*

Entranced. Captivated. Enchanted.

Connor sat across the table from Tori Jones and couldn't help thinking that those words exactly described what effect the small-town schoolteacher had on him. He might as well stop trying to tell himself he wasn't interested. He was powerfully drawn to her.

Clearly, he should have dated more when he was younger.

There had been a couple of other women since Jennifer had walked out on him. But he had never been entranced. Or captivated. Or enchanted.

Until now.

He wanted her—*her,* Tori Jones, in particular. Not just someone suitably attractive and well-bred, as Jennifer had been. Not just someone sophisticated, sexually exciting and discreet, which pretty much described the two women he'd dated after his marriage crashed and burned.

It came to him that he…he *liked* this woman. And that was new to him. He liked her quick wit, her wisdom and her big heart. He liked the passion in her voice when she talked about things she believed in.

He liked *her.* And suddenly it mattered all out of proportion that she might like him, too.

Was he losing it? He couldn't help but wonder. Was he cracking under the strain—of the soured economy, the McFarlane House setbacks, his divorce, the scary changes in his son? Of the changes he'd decided he needed to make in his life and himself?

Strangely, right then, on his first date with Tori Jones, he didn't care if he just might be going over the edge. He was having a great time—having *fun*, of all things—and he didn't want it to end.

Is Connor finally able to admit his feelings to Tori,
and are they reciprocated?
Find out in McFARLANE'S PERFECT BRIDE
by USA TODAY bestselling author Christine Rimmer.
Available July 2010,
only from Silhouette Special Edition®.

Top author

Janice Kay Johnson

*brings readers a heartwarming
small-town story*

with

CHARLOTTE'S HOMECOMING

After their father is badly injured on the farm,
Faith Russell calls her estranged twin sister,
Charlotte, to return to the small rural town she
escaped so many years ago. When Charlotte
falls for Gray Van Dusen, the handsome town
mayor, her feelings of home begin to change.
As the relationship grows, will Charlotte
finally realize that there is no better place
than *home*?

*Available in July
wherever books are sold.*